Shea sat on the edge of the bed as reality came slamming back.

Willing her pulse to steady, she took a deep breath in a desperate attempt to clear her head. Still giddy and a bit light-headed, her hand trembled as she ran her fingers through her hair. It had been close. Too close. His touch left her feeling badly in need of something more.

He hadn't made love to her. She should be monumentally happy. Why, then, did she feel ridiculously disappointed?

She'd almost had sex with Alec Morreston.

Even worse, he hadn't forced her. He hadn't held her down or tied her to the bedposts. He'd kissed her. That was all. Apparently, that had been enough. She knew it. And worse, so did he.

The full impact of that realization flooded her mind. Alec Morreston was here to take away her ranch, her home, everything she held dear. She would do well to remember that. He was, inarguably, a very potent package with obvious experience to back that up.

She had to be strong.

* * *

Dear Reader,

I've always loved the wide-open spaces of Texas and the true modern-day cowboys who are so much a part of the native culture. They have a will as strong and as spirited as the horses they ride. They share an ingrained toughness that weighs heavy against the two-thousand-pound bulls they challenge on a daily basis. They have hearts the size of the state in which they live, easy smiles and charisma you can sense from a mile away.

Alec is a native of New York, a rich city slicker used to a posh and relatively easy lifestyle. When suddenly faced with living on a five-thousand-acre ranch in the Lone Star State, he knows he has to step up his game in order to satisfy the *Terms of a Texas Marriage*. He doesn't foresee a problem—until the heroine presents challenges of a completely different nature.

I sincerely hope you will enjoy Shea and Alec's story. I love to hear from readers! Please drop me a note and check out upcoming releases by visiting my website, laurencanan.com.

Lauren Canan

TERMS OF A
TEXAS MARRIAGE

—

LAUREN CANAN

HARLEQUIN® DESIRE

Recycling programs
for this product may
not exist in your area.

ISBN-13: 978-0-373-73371-2

Terms of a Texas Marriage

Copyright © 2015 by Sarah Cannon

All rights reserved. Except for use in any review, the reproduction or utilization of this work in whole or in part in any form by any electronic, mechanical or other means, now known or hereafter invented, including xerography, photocopying and recording, or in any information storage or retrieval system, is forbidden without the written permission of the publisher, Harlequin Enterprises Limited, 225 Duncan Mill Road, Don Mills, Ontario M3B 3K9, Canada.

This is a work of fiction. Names, characters, places and incidents are either the product of the author's imagination or are used fictitiously, and any resemblance to actual persons, living or dead, business establishments, events or locales is entirely coincidental.

This edition published by arrangement with Harlequin Books S.A.

For questions and comments about the quality of this book, please contact us at CustomerService@Harlequin.com.

® and TM are trademarks of Harlequin Enterprises Limited or its corporate affiliates. Trademarks indicated with ® are registered in the United States Patent and Trademark Office, the Canadian Intellectual Property Office and in other countries.

HARLEQUIN®
www.Harlequin.com

Printed in U.S.A.

Lauren Canan, born and raised amid the cattle ranches of Texas, climbed a fence and jumped onto the back of her first horse at age three. She still maintains the punishment was worth the experience. She grew up listening to her dad tell stories of make-believe and was always encouraged to let her imagination soar. The multi-award-winning author and recipient of the 2014 Golden Heart® Award happily spends her days penning her favorite kind of stories: those of two people who, against all odds, meet, fall in love and live happily ever after—which is the way it should be. In her spare time she enjoys playing guitar, piano and dulcimer in acoustic club jams and getting lots of kisses and wags from her four-legged fuzzy babies. Visit Lauren's website at laurencanan.com. She would love to hear from you!

Books by Lauren Canan

Harlequin Desire

Terms of a Texas Marriage

I owe my love of telling stories to my dad. Without his inspiration and encouragement, my journey to become an author would never have begun. This story was possible because of the love and support of my critique siblings, Angi, Jan, Jen and Kathleen, who were always there with a shoulder to cry on when I needed one. To the best literary agent in the world, Jill Marsal, who has the patience of a saint. To my dearest friend, Laurel, whose belief in me never wavered. And to Terry, my own real-life hero. He taught me the true meaning of love and happily ever after.

One

Shea Hardin had to admit the man didn't look like the devil. No horns sprouted up through Alec Morreston's thick, expertly styled, mahogany-brown hair, although a few defiant tendrils fell lazily over his forehead. The wide mouth and well-defined lips, while appearing unrelenting, didn't make it to a complete snarl. The near-perfect white teeth, seen briefly in the forced smile as introductions were made, didn't include fangs. In fact, the sculpted features of his face had the potential to be exceedingly handsome, but the lack of any emotion other than cold indifference reduced that potential to tolerable. Just.

She'd sensed his glance several times since entering the conference room adjacent to her attorney's office. She didn't need to look in his direction to know he watched her, silently, recording his first impressions, probably sizing up her abilities, weighing her strengths, discreetly alert to any hint of weakness.

Feminine instinct told her his assessment wasn't limited to her ability to handle this situation. He was also taking in every curve of her body, noting every breath she took, watching every move she made. It was a frank and candid assessment of her female attributes without any effort to conceal his interest. Intuition told her here was a man who knew what a woman needed and exactly how to provide it. His subtle arrogance was at once insulting and alluring.

She tried to swallow but her mouth had gone dry. En-

deavoring not to appear affected by this man, she crossed
her legs, shook the hair back from her face and fixed her
eyes on the old pendulum wall clock. But in spite of her
determination to ignore him, there was no denying the heat
radiating throughout her body, inflaming her senses, fuel-
ing the unwanted need pooling in her lower belly.

Picking up a pencil, she scribbled furiously on the open
notepad. She was reacting like a besotted teenager. How
could she possibly feel any attraction whatsoever to this
man? His chosen path in life was destroying the past; tearing down the treasured remains of bygone eras, replacing
them with cold glass and steel fabrications. And this man
wanted her ranch. The awareness of her body's traitorous
response both stunned and angered her.

She was not going to be intimidated—or enticed—by
him or his attorney. The very reason they sat across from
her should be enough to dispel any thoughts that Alec Morreston would ever be someone she'd want to know better.

"If everyone is ready, I suggest we begin," said Ben
Rucker, her attorney and longtime family friend. He
switched on a small tape recorder sitting on the polished
conference table amid the varying papers, notepads and
legal documents.

"Today is April twenty-sixth. The purpose of this meeting is to address the issue of tenancy concerning the home
and land currently occupied by Shea Hardin. In attendance
are Alec Morreston, owner of the property, his attorney,
Thomas Long, Shea Hardin and myself, Ben Rucker, legal
counsel for Ms. Hardin."

Shea smiled at Ben. His tired but astute gray eyes reflected his concern over the situation. He'd practiced law
for almost forty years, and she had complete confidence
in his abilities, as her father had before her.

"At the turn of the nineteenth century, five thousand one
hundred and twenty acres of land running along the west-

ern boundary and into what is now the National Forest and Grassland Reserve in Calico County, Texas, were acquired by William Alec Morreston. Later that year, he transferred the entire parcel to a widow, Mary Josephine Hardin. Since that time, descendants of Mary Hardin have continued to live on the land, today licensed as the Bar H Ranch."

Ben reached for his glasses, placed them on his nose and picked up his copy of the original paperwork.

"Rather than a purchase, this transfer of land was handled in a manner similar to what we today call a lease." He glanced over the top of his glasses. "I believe you each have a copy of the original paperwork?" When everyone nodded, he continued. "You'll note the duration was ninety-nine years with a renewal option.

"The first lease term was renewed by Cyrus Hardin, Shea's great-grandfather. The second term, currently in effect, is due to expire at the end of this month—in five days, to be precise. Ms. Hardin would like to retain possession of the property. Mr. Morreston has indicated a desire to reclaim it for his own use. This can be achieved only if Ms. Hardin has not, or does not meet all of the renewal requirements by the end of the month."

Shea glanced at Alec Morreston and once again encountered the full intensity of his gaze. A powerful energy emanated from him, the full force of it focused directly on her. She swallowed hard and looked away, ignoring the increasing tempo of her pulse.

"We didn't inspect the house and outbuildings," Mr. Long advised without preamble. "But we are satisfied that everything appears in satisfactory condition. We concede all stipulations relating to the condition of the property have been met."

Shea closed her eyes as relief washed over her. Reaching out to Ben, she squeezed his arm and then looked at Mr. Long and Alec Morreston. So grateful they'd been honest in their findings, she even managed to send a stiff smile of thanks in his direction. He hesitantly tipped his head as if to say *you're welcome*, but she couldn't help but notice the raised eyebrow and the hint of a smirk in the hard lines of his face, almost as if he knew something she didn't.

Shea returned her attention to Ben. He wasn't smiling, and didn't appear to share in her feeling of relief. No one switched off the tape recorder. No one stood up. It was as though a silent warning had begun to flash in a quickly ascending elevator, indicating the bottom was about to drop out.

"In addition to the condition of the property," Ben said, still not meeting her glance. "Apparently the ancestors of Ms. Hardin and Mr. Morreston believed it necessary to add what I would describe as a personal clause."

"Personal clause?" Frowning, Shea began to page through her copy of the old, handwritten document.

"On page four, about two-thirds down the page." Ben removed his glasses and put down the paper as if he could recall the words from memory. His voice was quiet, his manner unusually gentle. "It states in addition to the actual upkeep, if the renewal of the lease is awarded to a woman, she must be legally wed by or before the expiration of the lease."

Her head snapped up, staring at Ben's face.

"What?" Her jaw dropped in astonishment. She frowned, not understanding or wanting to believe the implications of what she'd just heard.

"It further states—" Ben again donned the thick glasses and raised his chin, a motion that enabled him to use the lower, bi-focal portion of the lenses. "'If the female lessee has no husband or betrothed, the oldest adult male, unmarried, in the Morreston family will be joined to her in matrimony, legally and spiritually, and they shall live as husband and wife for a period of not less than one year to ensure her protection against any and all perils, assist her with all ranching endeavors and ensure she is given fair and equal consideration.

"'The failure of either party to meet these terms will result in the forfeiture of the property to the other. If a marriage does occur between the principal parties, such marriage can be terminated at the end of one year, and at such time the land will go to the Hardin family for another ninety-nine-year duration.'"

He sat back in his chair and tossed the documents onto the tabletop. "You gotta love the Morreston family chivalry."

Silence momentarily filled the small room.

"For what it's worth, Shea," Ben said, "I'd guess the families were very close, and this was their way of ensuring the safety of any woman who might be single and head of household when the lease expired. As you know, it used to be a man's world and a woman by herself didn't have much of a chance. The one year marriage provision was probably intended to ensure she had full support with the ranch. If either didn't want to stay married after that, they wouldn't be required to do so. Ironically—" his eyes narrowed as he looked at Alec Morreston "—the clause was probably intended to protect any female of the Hardin family from the *crooks* who might try and take advantage of her."

The only reaction from Alec Morreston was a deepening of the tiny lines around his eyes, a silent indication he found amusement in Ben's assessment.

"But…" Leaning forward, she placed her elbows on the table for support and rubbed her fingers against her temple, willing her brain to click back into gear. "You're saying… You're telling me the lease can't be renewed because I'm a single woman?"

"If I may," Thomas Long interjected. "What it means, Ms. Hardin, in the simplest terms, is that in order for you to renew the lease you must currently be married or you must agree to marry Alec within the next five days and remain married for at least one year. If you don't agree, the lease cancels. If Alec does not agree to such a marriage, should you choose that option, the lease will be renewed."

For a few moments, speech was impossible. Her eyes remained fixed on Mr. Long as her mind tried to make some sense out of his words. She was stupefied.

"You've *got* to be kidding. This is a sick joke. It's archaic." Although attempting to remain calm, her resolve was quickly slipping away. "This kind of thing isn't legal." She looked at Ben, who sat quietly, tapping his pencil on the tabletop. "Is it?"

Ben hesitated for a few seconds as if trying to formulate his answer. "As far as I've been able to determine, the owner of the property could place any clause, requirement or restriction in the lease that he wished within the existing laws of the time. If the lessee agreed, it became a binding agreement. As to the question of whether it's binding by today's laws, it may very well not be."

Hope flared within her.

"But the problem is, if we sue to have that clause stricken, the courts could declare the entire contract null and void, in which case Mr. Morreston is under absolutely no obligation to renew the lease. And, if the courts didn't find the clause unlawful, by the time they handed down their decision, the deadline would be past. Either way…" Ben made a small gesture with his hands, his palms turned upward, indicating the hopelessness of the situation.

Shea sat back in her chair and stared out the large picture window. How could such a beautiful spring day suddenly turn so bleak and ugly? She trained her eyes squarely on Alec Morreston.

"You knew about this, didn't you?"

"Yes," he replied, his voice deep and throaty. "Thomas caught it and advised me a couple of months ago. You might want to ask your attorney why he didn't see fit to inform you. Since he was obviously aware of your single marital status, it might have saved all of us a lot of time."

Her glance swung to Ben, who shrugged and shook his head. "I'm sorry, darlin'. I thought Mr. Morreston would view the outlandish clause for what it is. It never occurred to me he'd use it to his advantage to try and reclaim possession of the land."

"I don't believe it," she muttered. "I don't believe any of this. Are you all trying to tell me I've got to take this... *insanity* seriously? That I'm going to lose my home, my ranch, everything my father and his father before that worked for, because I'm not married and won't marry *him*?"

The tone in her voice clearly painted the "him" as something disgusting and vile—which, at that moment, was spot-on. In spite of his sexual charisma, her conscious mind told her Alec Morreston was nothing more than a cold-blooded opportunist. And as far as this...lease...how could anyone in his right mind possibly make up such a stipulation?

"Your loss was taken into consideration, Ms. Hardin." Alec pointedly ignored her outburst. His composed voice resonated through the thick silence that had temporarily blanketed the small room. "I'm willing to provide reimbursement for the structures on the property, including the house, as well as compensate for one year's ranch income. And, of course, the proceeds from the sale of your livestock and equipment will be yours, provided you choose to sell rather than relocate."

Shea glared at him, afraid to speak for fear it would release the torrent of fury welling up inside her. Comparing this man to the devil had been much too kind.

"In addition," Morreston continued, "I'm willing to provide adequate time for you to find another residence. We understand the relocation process will take longer than the standard sixty days."

"Alec is making a most generous offer, Ms. Hardin," added Thomas Long, as though he felt compelled to point that out.

Ignoring the attorney, she focused directly on the source of this insanity, on the devil incarnate. Sitting casually back in his chair, he appeared relaxed and completely indifferent to what amounted to the end of life as she knew it. Her basic principles, her education, her future dreams, pride in her family—all of it rested within the boundaries of the ranch. She couldn't imagine what her life would be without it.

"Why are you doing this?" Her voice was firm and unwavering, but her heart pounded and her stomach tied itself into knots.

"It's nothing personal, Ms. Hardin." He tipped his head to one side as his eyes roamed over her face. "It's just business."

"Oh, really?" she challenged. "That's what you call it? Destroying a person's life is 'just business?'" She shook her head in amazement. "You must think you'll make a small fortune on this deal."

"That's always a possibility," he admitted, shrugging his broad shoulders.

"I'm curious. What's it going to be? A dude ranch for your city friends or cheap housing that will fall apart in ten years?"

"I don't think Alec's future plans for the land need discussion at this—"

"It's good land in a prime location," Alec answered her, interrupting his attorney. "And the time for its development has come." His eyes never left her face, his tone hard and unemotional.

She couldn't help but speculate if they would have been

having this meeting if her dad were still alive. But common sense told her Morreston wanted the land and would have found other reasons to decline the renewal. This little "personal clause" was convenient and tailor-made to suit his purposes.

"You could omit the clause and renew the lease."

"I could," he admitted openly. "But I won't."

Silently she studied the hard, chiseled features of his face.

"Then there is no more to say, is there?" Standing, she gathered her papers and slipped them into the manila folder. She wouldn't grovel before any man, especially some arrogant stranger from New York, particularly when she knew it would do no good. Her hands were trembling due to shock, but she refused to let these contemptuous strangers see any weakness.

"Ben." She pressed her lips together to cover the trembling. "I assume you'll be in touch about what needs to be done?"

On seeing his nod, she gave a tight smile and walked out of the room. Somehow, she cleared the outside door without slamming it. Only when she reached the sidewalk did her vision blur with unshed tears of anger and frustration. Seven months ago, she'd buried her father. And now, in the space of less than an hour, she'd learned she was losing her home.

She swallowed back the overwhelming sense of panic. The ranch was her haven, her security. It was her past as well as her future. Her father had entrusted it to her care and she'd promised him in his final moments that his efforts—and the efforts of all the Hardins before them— would not be in vain.

She was the last, the only one remaining, who could carry the Hardin legacy into tomorrow. Two hundred years of struggle and sacrifice, of unwavering strength, bravery and determination by her forefathers to fashion a better life from this small piece of earth, and now, the future rested squarely on her shoulders. The weight of it was staggering.

Slipping behind the wheel of her old Chevy pickup, Shea tried recalling elements of the discussion. Even though Ben had conducted the meeting, she knew Alec Morreston had carefully orchestrated and controlled the entire presentation. Right down to her walking out of the room. The deliberate downplay of some factors of the contract, the strong focus on others. He was good. She had to give him that.

But there was one thing she'd bet Morreston hadn't taken into account. Her father had always said she was an obstinate, hardheaded female who never knew when to admit defeat. She had no intention of admitting failure so easily and giving in to that arrogant, money-grubbing son-of-a-bitch.

Maybe she would lose her home. But maybe she wouldn't.

Ben had said she must be married before the contract expired. He hadn't said she must be married to Alec Morreston, as his attorney had implied. Somewhere out there was a man who would agree to marry her for one year as a strictly business arrangement. She was going to find him.

She squared her shoulders with renewed conviction and started the truck. There was a lot to do and a very short time in which to do it.

Alec and Thomas gathered their respective documents and prepared to leave Ben Rucker's office. Ms. Hardin's abrupt exit from the meeting, while anticipated, had ended any further need for discussion.

Alec had to admit, he was impressed with Shea Hardin. She was not at all what he'd expected. In her midtwenties, she presented herself as having the maturity of someone much older. Even though this must have been devastating to her, she hadn't shouted or cried or otherwise made a scene as so many others in her position might have done.

She'd been upset, but that was understandable. Her parting words, quietly spoken to her attorney just before she'd left the room, indicated acceptance of the situation and what was to come.

But had she really given up? His success in business was due in large part to following his gut instincts. Rarely in his thirty-six years had those instincts let him down. Right now they were screaming that Shea Hardin had done anything *but* admit defeat.

From the top of the silky blond hair that fell in tousled disarray around her head to the tight jeans hugging her slim waist, then molding her sexy, feminine curves and long, slender legs, she was trouble with a capital T. If you added the delicate, almost angelic features of her face and the wide-eyed innocence of those amazing blue eyes, you had the makings of one hell of a problem. Shea Hardin would have no difficulty finding and persuading some spineless, misguided male to marry her for a year. She had five days to do it. And if she succeeded, he could kiss this project goodbye.

Alec regretted it had to be this way: that this young woman had to be forced out of her home. He'd experienced an uncomfortable twinge of regret even before her attorney had informed her of the hopelessness of her situation.

With a grimace, he tossed the last manila folder into his briefcase and closed it. Regret hadn't been the only thing he'd felt. He couldn't remember his libido ever reacting with the speed and intensity it had to Shea Hardin. A flash of insight told him sex with her would be hot and intense, mind-blowing in its fervor. Illogical anger flared at the idea of her marrying another man, lying in his bed. He shook his head to dispel the irrational notion. Under the circumstances, he'd be the last person on earth she'd ever let come near her.

As he snapped the locks on his briefcase closed, the idea

ran through his mind that he should find her, apologize for this seizure of the land and...what?

He wasn't backing away from this venture. He couldn't. Too much time and money already had been invested. So, what good would it do to apologize? She would soon be out of a home, and no apology would change that fact.

As they walked out of the building and toward the parking lot, Alec couldn't shake the idea that he shouldn't be leaving just yet. And if he was honest, he didn't know if it was concern about the land issue or a ridiculously illogical reluctance to walk away from Shea Hardin.

"Thomas," he said as they reached the car, "drop me off at the local car-rental agency, then drive back into Dallas, to Dallas-Fort Worth International, and go on to Boston. Meet with Rolston in the morning and finalize the plans for construction of his new hotel. You know what we need. Get the contracts signed, and I'll see you back in New York in a couple of days."

"You're staying here?" Thomas's brows rose in surprise. "You really think that's necessary?"

"Yeah. I have a feeling Ms. Hardin is not going to give in this easily."

"Well, keep me posted." Thomas opened the car door and tossed his suit coat inside. "Alec, don't start feeling bad about this woman's situation. You've offered her a lot of money that you didn't have to and you've given her virtually all the time she needs to relocate. Hell, it's *your* land."

"Yeah, I hear you." Alec nodded his head. "We're on the same page. I should be here only a couple of days. I'll call tonight and check on Scotty. Mom had the zoo scheduled for today. I have a feeling by now she should be about ready to go home."

"Your mother is keeping your son?"

Alec nodded. "Ms. Bishop quit. And after just two weeks, her replacement was already looking a bit frazzled." Alec shrugged. "Mother offered to come and stay with him. I flew her in from St. Petersburg just before we left to come here."

Thomas chuckled. "That boy is four going on twenty-four."

Alec smiled. "Don't I know it."

After arranging for a car, Alec eased the large sedan into the lane of traffic heading north. He should be on his way to Boston or back to New York. Instead, he was stuck in a rural north Texas town full of coyotes and cowboys, boots and brawls, dirt roads and bumper stickers proclaiming the South would rise again. He didn't belong here. He didn't want to be here. But he had to protect his right to this land. If it hadn't been mentioned in the reading of his grandfather's will, he wouldn't have known of its existence. Now that he knew, he wasn't about to let it slip through his hands.

The logical thing to do was to bring in a couple of his staff to keep an eye on things. But before the idea could begin to formulate, Shea Hardin's face drifted into his mind, and he squelched the plan before it had a chance to develop.

"Thanks for coming over, Leona." Shea pushed the screen door farther open, welcoming her neighbor onto the wide enclosed porch at the rear of the house. "I really do need your help."

Three days had passed since the meeting in Ben's office and Shea still hadn't come up with a solid plan to save the ranch.

"Are you all right?" Leona squinted and gave Shea a cursory inspection. "You sounded terrible on the phone. Kinda scared me. I was afraid you'd gotten kicked by that damn stallion again."

"I'm fine." She smiled at the older woman. "At least physically. Come on in and I'll fix us both a glass of tea."

Leona Finch was the closest thing to a mother figure Shea had since her own mom died when she was five. Shea loved Leona dearly. In her midsixties, the sun-browned features of her face bore the wrinkles of a lifetime spent on a working ranch. Her speech was as rough as her skin. But she was sensitive, perceptive and in spite of her limited education, profoundly wise.

"So, if you're not hurt, what's the deal?" Leona walked into the kitchen, pulled out a chair and sat down at the table as Shea filled two glasses with ice.

She poured the freshly brewed tea and added a sprig of mint. Setting the glasses on the table, she took a seat across from Leona.

"I've…I've got a problem," she began. "A big one."

"Well, hell." Leona took a sip of the tea and sat back in the chair. "There ain't a problem that can't be fixed. You tell me what's got you so upset, and then we'll figure out how to put it right."

Shea gave her friend a strained smile. She was glad to have Leona on her side. She needed to hear a few of her unceasingly positive assurances that things would work out.

"I'm not sure exactly where to begin. Three days ago I was called to a meeting in Ben's office. It's so bizarre…" Her voice trailed off as she shook her head. Shea looked into her friend's face.

"It seems I've got to find a husband," she told Leona straight out. "And I have less than two days left to do it."

Two

"You've got to do *what*?" Leona leaned forward and Shea saw her eyes narrow as she searched for any sign of a joke.

Shea took a steadying sip of tea. "If I don't get married by the last day of this month, I'll lose the ranch."

"Says who?" Leona's tone was guarded.

Shea recounted the highlights of the meeting in Ben Rucker's office three days earlier. She still had a hard time believing it herself.

"I have no intention of just walking away from everything I love and everything Dad worked so hard to accomplish." Her finger made circles in the condensation forming on the frosted glass. "I've spent the last three days on the phone trying to track down some of my friends from college. The ones I did manage to locate are married or involved with someone. Between the years I was away at school and then Dad's illness, I've lost touch with most of the people I knew in high school."

There had been two loves in her life. The first had been a high school crush who was now married with two kids. She'd met the other, David Rollins, her second year in college. For a while, they had been inseparable and even had talked about marriage. But eventually they both had realized they wanted different things in life. David's plans hadn't included living on a ranch in north Texas. Shea hadn't been able to see herself living anywhere else. She'd tried desperately to reach David, but without any luck. A few of her friends had heard he was living back East, but no one knew exactly where. Some had offered to make calls to try to reach him, but so far he hadn't called.

She pulled a legal pad from under some *Western Horsemen* magazines that lay on the table. "I've made a list of a few possibilities, but—" she shook her head in frustration as she passed the pad to Leona "—it's been a long time."

Leona took the list and set it aside, her eyes locked on Shea's face. "You're not seriously thinking about asking some man to marry you." It was more a statement than a question.

She shrugged. "What else can I do?"

"Do you have even the slightest idea what you'd be letting yourself in for?"

"It will be a business agreement, strictly platonic."

"Yeah, sure it will," Leona muttered, rubbing her hand over her face. "God Almighty. This is the damnedest situation I've ever heard of."

Leona picked up the list, gave her a weary look and began to scan the names. "Tommy Hall. Are his parents John and Grace?"

"Yeah." Shea nodded.

"He got married two weeks ago. One of our hands was his best man." Leona picked up a pen and crossed off his name.

"Duncan Adams. Drinks," she recalled. "A lot. You don't need that grief. Cecil Taylor? I hear he loses more than he makes on the horses over in Bossier City. Unless you're willing to bankroll his gambling, you can scratch him off the list."

One by one, Leona crossed off each man until, of the fourteen names, only one remained.

"What about Tim Schultz?" Shea asked, trying not to sound desperate.

Leona looked at the last name on the list. "Maybe. Isn't

his father the preacher over at that little church east of town?" She frowned in contemplation. "I've never heard nothing bad about him. Kinda quiet. 'Bout your age, right?"

"Yeah," Shea confirmed. "His family only moved to this area a few years ago, but I had some classes with him in college. He's nice enough, I guess."

"So, how do you plan to approach him with this little plan of yours?" Leona laid the pen and pad on the table. "You gonna just walk up to him and say, 'Howdy. Will you marry me for a year? Oh, and by the way, it's strictly business.' I'd sure like to be a fly on the wall when you throw that little tidbit in his direction."

"I'll explain the circumstances, of course." She hadn't rationalized this part of the plan, but obviously it would be necessary. "I'll have to."

"Girl, use your head. Maybe if you talked to that Morreston fellow again—"

"No." Sitting back in her chair, Shea crossed her arms in front of her. Alec Morreston. The mere mention of his name caused a hot blush to spread over her neck and face. The look of male want in his eyes was still vivid in her mind. She'd never experienced anything like it, but even after three days, she knew she hadn't imagined it. And neither had she imagined his cold insensitivity to the havoc he'd caused in her life. She resolutely shook her head. "I can promise you, it would do no good. He's a developer. He lives in New York, probably in some posh penthouse. He doesn't care about the land. He doesn't care about anything but making more money. Probably never got his hands dirty in his life."

"What if you turned the tables on him?" Leona asked, taking another long drink of her tea.

Shea frowned. "I don't understand."

"Well, Ben told you, according to that contract, if you

weren't married by the end of the month, Morreston had to marry you or agree to renew the lease. Right?"

Shea nodded, suddenly afraid of where this was going.

"So tell him you want to marry him."

Shea could only gape in horror.

"Put the problem back on his plate," Leona reasoned. "Think about it. He's a city fellow. He's not going to agree to marry you and live on this ranch. He thinks he's got you bluffed into doing just exactly what you're doing— refusing to use him as a way out."

Shea stubbornly shook her head. "No way, Leona." The idea was beyond bizarre. "Absolutely no way." She still had forty-eight hours.

"I sure wish your father was still alive," Leona muttered.

"So do I, Leona," Shea whispered as she stood and walked to the phone to call Tim Schultz. "So do I."

Shea sipped from the glass of ice water and tried to remain calm. Tonight, before midnight, she had to be married. Tim had finally returned her call this morning. No doubt sensing the urgency in her tone, he'd agreed to meet her at Barstall's City Diner at one o'clock. He was late.

What was she going to say? All the rehearsing in the world couldn't prepare her for what she had to discuss with him. How would he respond? Would he laugh? Would he just walk out? Or, most important, would he agree to do it?

Before leaving yesterday, Leona once more had encouraged her to call Morreston's bluff. But Shea had held firm in her conviction that nothing on earth would make her so desperate to even contemplate such a thing. Heaven help the poor female coerced into marriage with that man.

Instinctively she knew Alec Morreston would be demanding, in bed as well as out. Even if the situation were different, a brief affair with a man like Morreston would take more from her than she could give. She suspected such a liaison would turn into an emotional roller coaster, and that was the last thing she needed in her life.

But it was a moot point. Morreston was long gone. It had taken him fewer than two hours to invade her world and turn it completely upside down. Then he had left, not even bothering to look back as she desperately tried to pick up the pieces from the devastation he'd caused. No doubt, he assumed she would just relinquish her home and quietly disappear. Well, he was in for a surprise—

"Hello, Ms. Hardin." Shea jumped at the sound of the deep voice directly to her left. Her head snapped around and her eyes immediately grew wide in astonishment. She could feel the blood drain from her face as she stared into the amber eyes of Alec Morreston.

"May I join you?"

Before she could respond, he pulled out the chair opposite her and sat down. As his eyes scanned her face, his lips twitched with unrepressed humor at her stunned look. For a long moment, she couldn't speak.

"What…what are you doing here?" she stammered, finally finding her voice.

"I'm about to have lunch," he said innocently, as though misunderstanding the true meaning of her question.

Shea glared at him.

Alec shrugged. "I decided to take a few days and see some of the area. Thought it might be…beneficial…to the future development of the project." He responded as if choosing his words carefully. "Have you ordered yet?"

"Have I…? No." She shook her head. "No. I'm meeting someone." She looked toward the front entrance, no longer sure she'd be glad to see Tim walk through it.

Alec regarded her silently for a moment. "I see. Well, then I'll certainly move to another table as soon as she— or he?—arrives."

If Shea had been nervous before Morreston's unexpected

arrival, that feeling was mild compared to what she was experiencing now. Suddenly, she could relate to every mouse ever caught in a trap that had looked up to find the cat walking in its direction. How on earth was she ever going to present her problem to Tim with Morreston hanging over her shoulder?

"The roasted chicken sounds good," he commented, scanning the lunch specials. "What do you recommend?"

"You really don't want me to answer that."

He glanced at her face over the top of the menu and feigned surprise. But the deepening of the tiny lines around his eyes told her he found her remark amusing.

Before she could deliberate on this newest chapter of the nightmare, another voice beckoned her.

"Um…excuse me. Shea?" Tim Schultz smiled his apology. "Sorry I'm late."

"Tim!" She smiled nervously. "That's okay."

She looked back to Morreston, hoping against hope he would just silently disappear. Apparently, that was not going to be the case. Politeness demanded she make introductions.

"Tim, this is Alec Morreston…Tim Schultz."

Alec stood as the two men shook hands. Over six feet in height, he easily towered over the younger man by several inches while his broad shoulders and lean waist hinted at a muscular, athletic build that made Tim appear almost adolescent in comparison. His reddish-blond hair and fair complexion seemed pale, almost sickly, as opposed to Morreston's dark features.

"Well, if you'll excuse me," Alec said, a grin tugging at the corners of his well-defined mouth, "I'm sure you two have a great deal to discuss. I certainly don't want to interrupt."

"Would you care to join us?" Tim asked, unaware of the situation.

"No!" Shea almost shrieked. Both men looked at her—one with curiosity, the other with increasing amusement.

"Thanks, Tim," Alec said, and Shea's heart all but stopped. "But I think Shea wants to speak privately with you. Maybe another time?"

He knows. He knows exactly why I'm having lunch with Tim Schultz. And apparently, he found the situation extremely amusing. That infamous smirk was firmly in place.

"You knew I was here, didn't you?" It was no coincidence Alec Morreston just happened to show up at the exact time she was meeting with Tim, even if it was the lunch hour and this was the only decent restaurant in town. When he didn't immediately respond, she added, "How?"

"I believe his name is Hank. Your ranch foreman? He said you might be having lunch here today."

Alec moved away from their table, giving her a quick wink as if to seal the private joke between them. She immediately turned away, biting back the angry retort that sprang to her lips. *Ignore him*, she told herself. *Just be thankful to be rid of him.*

But before she could enjoy a second of relief, to her utter dismay, Morreston pulled out a chair at a table next to them. In that location he'd be able to hear every word they said. Something akin to panic formed in her stomach.

"So," Tim began as he took the seat Alec had occupied. "How are you, Shea? Haven't seen you in what—three years? I was surprised to get your call. What's going on?"

She forced a smile and reached for the glass of ice water, needing something to steady her nerves. Her hand shook slightly, and a small amount of water spilled onto the table. As she fought to find the right words, her gaze wavered, and she found herself looking directly into the mocking face of Alec Morreston.

"Shea?"

She heard Tim's voice, but her gaze was captured by amber eyes.

"Shea? Is something wrong?"

She couldn't suppress the overwhelming desire to slam something as she stomped out of the restaurant. She was furious. No, she mentally corrected herself. She was beyond furious. She wanted to kill something. She wanted to kill Alec Morreston.

Each time she'd broached the subject of her meeting with Tim, Morreston had cleared his throat or apologetically interrupted to ask Tim a question or made some asinine comment. Between his little interruptions, he'd sat back in his chair and stared, never taking his eyes off her, exactly as he'd done that first day in Ben's office. That knowing smirk had remained etched on his lips, his tawny eyes alert to every movement she'd made, every breath she'd taken. For almost an hour, he'd made her feel like a bug under a microscope.

About the time she'd started to ask Tim if he would walk her to the truck, Morreston had folded his napkin, placed it on the table and leaned toward her lunch date to strike up a conversation. If they'd tried to leave, she'd known Morreston would have followed. Pleading a headache, she'd excused herself and asked Tim if she could call him later.

Now apprehension increased with each step as she made her way to her vehicle. Her time was almost up. It was down to a few short hours before she would lose the home she loved forever. She'd almost been tempted to stand in the center of the restaurant, loudly declare her problem and ask if there were any takers. If she didn't come up with a plan very soon, it just might come to that.

As she drove toward the parking lot exit, the front doors of the restaurant swung open and out walked Morreston— with Tim at his side. Seemingly engaged in light banter, only Morreston noticed her as she passed. He tipped his head to her in silent acknowledgment. She clutched the steering wheel in a death grip. Her hands itched to slap that arrogant smirk from his face once and for all. In the rearview mirror, she saw him turn to Tim, nod and laugh.

In that moment, she knew she never would have a second chance to speak with Tim. Morreston would see to it. That was why he was here. He knew what she was attempting to do, and he was determined to see her fail. The devil had just sprouted horns.

In the same instant, she also knew she'd reached the limit of her patience with the man and this bizarre situation. She slammed on the brakes and, without pausing to give her actions a second consideration, threw the truck into Reverse. It quickly roared backward before grinding to a halt directly in front of the two men. Their conversation immediately stopped and they both peered at her with curiosity.

She rolled down the window, a phony smile pasted to her lips. Alec watched her with guarded interest.

"Sorry to interrupt you gentlemen. But, *Alec*—?" She used his given name, implying a familiarity that was not there and never would be if she had anything to say about it. She gave him a look of pure innocence.

"You know, I've had a chance to think about our meeting earlier in the week. About the little problem we discussed?"

She had his attention.

"And, well, I think your attorney was right when he pointed out your family's unwavering concern that a single, unmarried woman can't possibly run a ranch…all by herself." The sarcasm dripped from her voice. Her tone was venomous.

Tim looked from one of them to the other, as if struggling to understand any part of their conversation.

"Since Mr. Long was so kind as to explain my alternatives and well…since you've gone to all the trouble to stay here in case I needed you, and in light of all the care and understanding you've shown, I think you're absolutely right." She looked directly into the golden depths of his eyes, an effort that challenged her sanity. "I will marry you, Alec. Under the circumstances, how can I possibly refuse?"

Only Alec comprehended the true meaning of her words. His head drew back, his eyes narrowed and her phony smile almost became genuine as she saw the flare of annoyance in those chiseled features.

"If you'll meet me at Ben Rucker's office in, oh, about an hour? I'm sure he can help us sort out any little details we need to address prior to the ceremony."

Before she switched her attention to Tim, she noted with satisfaction that the smirk was finally, effectively wiped from Morreston's face.

"Tim, I'm sorry I didn't have a chance to discuss this with you inside," she apologized. "But my reason for asking you here was to solicit your help in convincing your father to perform the ceremony on such short notice. Would you mind speaking to him for me?" She surprised herself at how quickly and convincingly the lie rolled off her tongue.

"No," Tim shrugged. If he believed this conversation to be as bizarre as it sounded, he managed to hide it well. "I'll see him this afternoon. When is the wedding? And where?"

"This evening. At my house." Her eyes returned to Alec's face and she noted, with immense gratification, he clearly showed signs of irritation. His jaw worked convulsively as he made a futile attempt to remain calm.

"Will eight o'clock be all right?" she asked.

For a long moment, Alec didn't answer. His eyes searched her face as if attempting to discern what she was up to, as though he couldn't believe what she had just said.

"Eight will be fine," he said finally.

If he'd refused, she'd have been surprised. She knew

instinctively that Morreston was not the type of person to back down after the first stone was cast.

She put the truck in Drive and smiled at Alec. His amber eyes narrowed in a silent declaration of war. While she suspected her triumph would be short lived, it would certainly feel good while it lasted.

"I can't let you do this," Ben Rucker stated for the third time. "Suppose the man doesn't refuse to marry you? What then?"

"Then we'll get married," she said firmly. "At eight this evening. Don't worry, Ben, you're invited."

"This is not a joke!" Ben pulled the glasses off his face and stood up from the desk. "For God's sake, don't do this, Shea. Take the money he's offered and buy land elsewhere. I'll help you. You can—"

"No, Ben. This is my home, my family home, for six generations. I can't just pack up two hundred years of memories and close that door behind me saying, 'Oh well.' If Morreston wants this land, *my* land, he'll have to fight for it."

Ben's eyes, full of concern, silently beseeched her to reconsider. "Is there no way I can talk you out of this?"

"Not unless Alec Morreston will renew my lease."

"Which he is not willing to do." The deep voice responded from the open doorway just behind her. Both Shea and Ben looked around in time to see the subject of their conversation walk casually into the room.

He had shed the sports jacket and tie, leaving his shirt open at the neck but still tucked into the navy slacks. They hugged his slim waist, hinting at muscular thighs beneath the fabric. Somehow, his shoulders seemed broader than they had only an hour ago. The strong line of his jaw was set in determination.

"Don't do this, Morreston," Ben pleaded.

"It's not completely my doing," he answered. His eyes focused on Shea. "Ms. Hardin had a choice, and apparently she decided on this option."

"You gave her no choice at all and you know it," Ben argued. "What kind of man are you to take advantage of her like this?"

Alec pointedly ignored the question. "I'd like to speak with Ms. Hardin in private." His eyes never left her face.

"You can discuss anything that needs saying in front of—"

"No, Ben. It's all right," Shea interrupted. This was her battle now. If she had any hope of making Morreston back down, she couldn't do it hiding behind her attorney. "Shall we step into the next room, Mr. Morreston?"

Alec followed her into the small, adjacent conference room and closed the door behind them with a resounding click. For a few moments they faced each other in silence.

"Are you really serious about this?"

"Yes," Shea replied without hesitation. "I am."

"You would marry a complete stranger in order to keep the land?"

"Yes."

"There is other land."

"Then perhaps you should go and find it."

Alec stared at her. "How much more do you want?" he asked quietly.

Had this man never loved anything in his life that didn't have a price tag attached to it? Could he not understand the legacy she was fighting to save?

"Two million," she said flippantly, and immediately saw a knowing look cross his face. The slight nod of his head indicated his initial acceptance of her outlandish but bogus demand. She was tempted to see how far he would go to buy her off but common sense came rushing forward.

"I don't want your money, Mr. Morreston. This is not

about money. It's about my home. My life. Family values and tradition. Things you, apparently, don't know anything about."

He shoved his hands into the pockets of his slacks and walked past her to stand gazing out the large window on the opposite wall. For long moments, he stood there, saying nothing. From the corner of her eye, she watched as he rubbed the back of his neck. His shirt did little to hide the muscular tone of his arms and back. The silky texture of his dark hair caught the subtle light coming through the window, accentuating deep auburn highlights. As he turned toward her, she quickly looked away.

"It won't work, you know." His voice had a slight raspy quality, which, under different circumstances, she might have found extremely sensual. "Even if I agree to this, no marriage can survive for a year under these circumstances. Eventually you'll concede defeat and the land will revert to me. It's inevitable. Why put yourself through it?"

"That's a very chauvinistic attitude, Mr. Morreston. What makes you so sure *I'll* be the one to call it quits?"

He didn't immediately answer as a look of indulgent amusement crossed his features. Then all traces of humor disappeared. Slowly, he closed in until barely a foot separated them. Without any warning, he reached out and stroked the side of her face.

She inhaled sharply and adjusted her stance at the unexpected contact but determinedly held her ground. His hand slid from her face to cup the back of her neck and, applying the slightest pressure, drew her even closer to him. She watched his gaze roam over each detail of her face before coming to rest on her mouth. She noted the faint shadow that darkened his face as he bent his head toward her. His lips, wide and defined, parted slightly as if intending to kiss her, but stopped a mere breath away, and only his thumb touched her mouth, tracing the curving fullness in an incredibly intimate gesture.

Time stood still. The close physical contact brought her challenge into clear focus. The pulse hammered in her throat. She swallowed back the overwhelming sensation of panic that rose within her and tried to look away.

Alec gently tilted her chin upward, forcing her to look into the golden depths of his eyes. The bittersweet fragrance of his cologne teased her senses. She could sense the disciplined power and virility of his body as he stood mere inches away from her. There was no doubt he was all male. Her stomach muscles involuntarily contracted as a shaft of sexual awareness shot through her. An intense heat seemed to envelop her as her breath became shallow, almost nonexistent. A little voice inside screamed to run while she could.

Three

"All right, Ms. Hardin." His throaty voice penetrated the silence of the room. "We'll play this one your way and see what happens. I'll honor the conditions as set forth by our ancestors and we will be married. And there will be no development on any of the land as long as the marriage continues or if this…union…should exceed one year."

He paused, tilting his head slightly as though studying her reaction. "But know this—" the tone of his voice reflected the seriousness of his words "—you *will* be my wife as stipulated in the original lease. Legally and spiritually, body and soul. You'll share my life, as well as my bed, for the duration. Do you understand what I'm saying?"

It was time to bail out. She knew it but couldn't seem to move. He was telling her exactly what she would have to agree to, up front. He was giving her every opportunity to walk away. She took a deep breath and hoped her strength was as unfailing as her stubbornness.

"I understand." Her voice was firm although barely above a whisper.

"Do you?" A sparkle glistened in Alec Morreston's amber eyes. "I guess we'll find out tonight, won't we?"

He released her and stepped toward the door but hesitated before pulling it open. "One more thing. I'll require a prenuptial agreement. Thomas should have time to fax one to your attorney's office before—"

"No."

His eyes narrowed, pinning her to the spot. "Excuse me?"

"You heard me. I said no."

"Ms. Hardin, do you really expect me to marry a woman I don't know and risk losing half of everything I have?"

"I'd say, after your earlier statement, you expect me to give up more than that. No prenup, Mr. Morreston. I want no part of anything you own, other than my ranch. You can trust me on that—" Shea eyed him coolly "—or you can book your flight home."

She could see the muscles in his jaw working overtime as he apparently strove to keep his temper from exploding.

"My personal holdings have nothing to do with this land issue. If, as you say, you want nothing but the land, then signing a prenup should not be asking too much."

"Neither is wanting to keep my home," she countered. "Nothing in the contract said anything about a prenuptial agreement. I refuse to sign one. If you refuse to marry me because of that, then I guess the land is mine. Your call."

Her heart beat so solidly against the wall of her chest she felt sure he could hear it from three feet away. She hoped she looked calmer on the outside than she felt on the inside.

Silence dominated the room. A barely perceivable change in his stance, from tense to an almost exaggerated casualness, conveyed the control he maintained on his emotions. His tawny eyes drifted over her as if trying to discover how much determination lay underneath. The burning strength of his gaze wandered insolently from her face to her breasts, down to her belly, to her hands—held tightly clenched at her sides—then down the legs of her jeans all the way to her feet. Shea could feel the blush spread across her face as he rudely inspected and silently weighed the feminine merchandise standing in front of him.

"All right, Ms. Hardin," he said finally, his tone suddenly menacing. "We'll play hardball if that's what you want. You just upped the stakes and I'd be a fool not to call your bluff. Be ready tonight, honey. Be ready for me."

He stepped back and opened the door. Shea shakily, but resolutely, walked through it. While temporarily disconcerted by his unexpected and candid proclamation, she knew the marriage would never be consummated. He was trying to intimidate her. That's all it was. He would do well to remember that two could play this game.

She had no intention of letting herself become physically ensnared and used by an egotistical maniac. She may have been forced into making a pact with the devil, but he would quickly find she was anything but a sacrificial lamb. Alec Morreston was city bred and raised. He had no concept of the sometimes harsh realities of ranch life, and she'd bet he wouldn't last a month.

In fact, she had just bet the ranch on it.

"Alec..." The heavy concern in Thomas's voice was clearly evident through the telephone line. Alec could picture him gripping the receiver so tightly his knuckles were turning white. He was almost sorry he couldn't be there in person to deliver the news of the pending wedding. "Are you certain you know what you're doing?"

Because their client-attorney relationship had grown into a solid friendship over the years, Alec wasn't insulted when Thomas questioned his sanity. Hell, in the past five hours, he'd begun to question it himself.

"I mean, what do we really know about this woman?"

"I think she's okay, Thomas."

"But what if she's not? What if this is all a setup? Do you have to *marry* her, for God's sake?" His tone was incredulous. "Maybe if you offered her more money?"

"She wouldn't take two million."

"She—" Alec heard Thomas Long swallow hard on that one. "My God! How much more does she want?"

"She says she doesn't want money. She wants the land. I believe, in her mind, she's telling the truth. She honestly thinks she can pull this off and make me back down. Unfortunately for her, I've committed to building this entertainment complex. The investors are already on board. I'm down several million and we haven't yet poured the first foundation. There is no turning back at this point."

"How about we try to find other land alternatives. I could put out some feelers…"

"A friend who specializes in real estate spent almost a year doing just that. I originally wanted to build in the East. He checked land possibilities within a hundred-mile radius of every major city near a natural waterway from New York to Florida. We encountered zoning restrictions, municipal politics, arbitrary city codes, small town gluttony. He found a two-thousand-acre tract just outside Cincinnati, but the deed was in probate. There was a five-thousand-acre tract in Virginia, but it was so far removed from civilization I didn't want to take the chance it might be *too* far.

"This location is perfect. A little farther west than I initially wanted, but it's actually working out even better than the original plan. It's centrally located in the US, only fifty miles from the Dallas-Ft. Worth International Airport and it borders the Red River."

Alec had already purchased land directly across the state line in Oklahoma and had most of the permits for that side of the river. "I've spent weeks restructuring blueprints to meet local building codes, obtaining land surveys for two states and finally have received a clearance from the EPA over some near-extinct bird they thought nested nearby. I refuse to spend any more time or money trying to find equivalent land just so Ms. Hardin can continue to raise her cows. Give me a few days, a couple of weeks at best, and I'll have her out of here."

"Okay." There was a moment of silence while Thomas,

no doubt, regrouped. "What about a prenup? You're potentially handing this woman a key to a very large door. Your bank accounts alone…" Thomas paused. "I'll have a basic agreement drawn up and sent to you in—"

"No thanks, Thomas."

"*No?* Alec—"

"We've already had this discussion. She refused."

Another stunned silence. "Then don't marry her. Let her have the damn land. Even considering how much you've sunk into the project, it isn't worth a fraction of your other holdings. Alec—"

"Thomas, look, I appreciate your concern. But I honestly feel if it should come down to a divorce petition for any of my current assets, the bizarre reason for the marriage—my being forced to take this route in order to regain the use of my own land—would supersede any claim."

"But we can't know that for sure."

How could he explain to Thomas his gut instinct said this would not be a problem? There was something about Shea Hardin, some glimmer of truth deep in those blue eyes. Nothing he'd seen gave him any reason to suspect she wanted any more than *her* ranch.

"I don't intend to remain married for one millisecond longer than absolutely necessary. In less time than it would take to battle this out, I intend to have her bags packed and be helping little Miss Tradition out the door. Then a simple annulment, give her something for her trouble, and it's done."

He'd been challenged by opponents a lot tougher than Shea Hardin and had come out on top. He grimaced at his own expression. Hell, in truth, on top of her was exactly where he wanted to be. He sensed the blood congregate in his loins at the mental picture and cursed his weakness. He had to keep his focus on the reason he was here and stop letting his imagination run wild.

Alec intentionally changed the subject. "I need you to call Valturego. See if he's ready to sign the contract for the construction of his casino. I'll contact him when I get back in the office."

"I'll call as soon as we're finished," Thomas promised. "But, Alec, back to the prenup thing—"

"Did Rolston sign the revised contract?"

Thomas grudgingly took the hint and began explaining the outcome of his meeting with the banker.

When their business concluded, Alec tossed his cell on the bed in the small motel room and glanced at the digital clock on the nightstand. After six. He probably should start getting ready.

The last time he'd taken vows, there had been more than fifteen hundred invited guests—some he'd known, most he hadn't. The planning had gone on for months. The fragrance from thousands of flowers had permeated the air, almost overwhelming the guests who'd gathered in the enormous church. He could remember the aura of hushed excitement that had filled the large sanctuary in anticipation of the spectacle to come.

Sondra had wanted it all and she had been relentless in making her desires come true. In hindsight, he should have seen what was coming. He should have picked up on the clues. She'd loved to party and her actions had made him suspect she'd crossed the line as far as using drugs. But he hadn't been able to prove it, had never found any evidence, and he'd never known about the other man until the day he came home and found the note. No excuses. No apologies. A strange woman waiting outside his door handed him a baby and said it was his. Suddenly he was alone with an infant son. A month later, Alec learned she'd died of an overdose. The man she'd left him to be with supposedly had provided the pills.

In the years since, the anger over her betrayal had diminished, but the lesson she'd taught him about trust had reshaped his character and would always be foremost in his mind. He'd sworn he would never again make the mistake of marrying. Anyone. For any reason. For almost five years, he'd kept that resolution. But in less than an hour, he would once again stand in front of a minister and make a pledge to love, honor and obey, and this time to a woman he knew nothing about.

Shea Hardin was a total perplexity. She didn't fit into any mold he'd ever come across. At first, he'd believed she was one of the members of Gold Diggers Anonymous he frequently encountered. But if those initial suspicions were correct, she was better than average at setting a trap, because he'd certainly taken the bait. She came across as completely sincere, candid and unwavering in her determination to keep the land.

She was a walking contradiction—intelligent yet naive, beautiful but unsophisticated, sexy as hell yet seemingly innocent. She looked fragile, sensitive, as though her poise and conviction could easily be shattered. But after today, he had the solid impression she was about as fragile as an oak tree, her temper as controlled as a glass vile of nitroglycerin.

She challenged him. She fascinated him.

And she had the most amazing blue eyes he'd ever seen.

Then there was her mouth—full lips that could give a man all kinds of grief, all kinds of pleasure. He'd almost kissed her in the attorney's office, drawing back at the last minute as he realized he wouldn't have wanted to stop with a single kiss.

No, his problem would not be intimidating Shea Hardin. It would be keeping himself from taking her while he did so.

Shea stood in front of her closet later that afternoon, staring at the few dresses hanging inside. Rarely was there any need for her to wear anything other than casual ranch attire and therefore her options were severely limited. She removed a simple paisley dress from the closet and held it in front of her as she viewed her reflection in the full-length mirror. Somehow, it didn't seem right.

She replaced it and reached for another. Wrong style. She bit her lip as she removed a dark green suit from the closet. Not right either. Red? Nope. Black? An impish grin crossed her face at the picture that would create. Quelling the urge, she hung the dress back in the closet and shook her head in frustration. There was no time to go shopping. Under the circumstances she should probably just pull on a clean pair of jeans and be done with it.

Thinking back on her day, she couldn't believe how fast everything had fallen into place for this wedding. Old Doc Hardy had done the blood work on the spot and Jane Simmons at the courthouse had gotten Judge Lamb to push the license through without the three-day wait. It was as unbelievable as her reason for being there.

Suddenly the mirror's reflection caught the motion of a large ball of orange fur as Pumpkin, the old tomcat, jumped onto the cedar chest that sat at the foot of her bed. She spun around and looked at the chest in speculation. Instantly memories of her childhood came rushing back. Memories of her as a little girl standing on top of the chest, trying to be tall enough so she could wear the long silky white dress her mother kept inside. It had been years since she'd reflected on the chest and its contents. On a whim, she set a disgruntled Pumpkin on the floor and then moved the miscellaneous items on top of the chest. A mild scent of cedar permeated the air around her as she raised the lid.

On top were pillowcases, handkerchiefs and small hand towels, their borders bearing floral designs embroidered by her mother. With a regretful smile, Shea set the linens aside. Underneath were two handmade quilts, their colors still amazingly crisp. She noted a date sewn into the corner of one: "A.H.—1812". Her great-grandmother must have made them. Maybe even her grandmother before that. She placed them on the floor next to the linens.

Kneeling over the now half-empty chest, she removed several more layers of tissue paper. Suddenly, there it was, and just as she remembered. Her mother's wedding gown. She rose to her feet as she lifted it out of the chest.

The material was an off-white satin. The years had slightly darkened the creamy color, but time couldn't diminish its simple elegance. The high, Victorian-style neckline, enhanced by delicate lace, covered the bodice and shoulders. Tiny pearl buttons ran down the full length of the gown with a matching row of buttons on each sleeve from the wrist to the elbow.

Tears stung her eyes as she was suddenly overcome with longing for the mother she'd never really known. She gently touched the delicate lace. Should she dare risk tarnishing the memory of her mother's wedding day by wearing it to the marital atrocity about to take place? But the thought of putting it back in the trunk and closing the lid didn't feel right. Something urged her to try it on.

Some ten minutes later, she stepped in front of the mirror and almost didn't recognize her reflection. The gown fit perfectly. Its simple style subtly created an aura of poise and sophistication as it gracefully cascaded to the floor.

She caught her lower lip between her teeth. Sadly, she wished hers would be a genuine marriage, one based on love and respect with hopes for a future. Not a contractual stipulation with an arrogant stranger.

Alec Morreston would no doubt have a good laugh if she appeared in a wedding gown. He'd be convinced she was every kind of crazy. She chewed her bottom lip. When she walked into the room for the ceremony would she feel like a total and complete fool? Circumstances being what they were, it probably was an idiotic idea. Still, a woman got married for the first time only once in her life. Right or wrong, this was it.

There was also the chance Morreston might think she was trying to play him and raise his guard, which could make getting rid of him more difficult. She let out a frustrated sigh. Wearing her mother's gown was fulfilling a dream she'd carried since childhood. If he laughed, why should she care? Let him scoff all he wanted, the hateful man.

"You know what, Pumpkin? Bizarre or not, this *is* my wedding day. I'm going to do it." As soon as she uttered the words, she knew she was making the right decision. There would be just enough time to freshen the dress before Morreston and the Reverend Shultz arrived.

But first, she needed to have a talk with Hank Minton, the ranch foreman. Quickly, she undressed, placed the gown on the bed and then pulled on a pair of jeans before heading for the main barn.

Four

"Do you, William Alec Morreston, take this woman as your lawfully wedded wife, to have and to hold from this day forward, for better or worse, for richer or poorer, in sickness and in health?"

Shea's head swam. This couldn't be happening. Perhaps if she blinked her eyes fast enough she would awaken from the nightmare.

Standing next to her in the old-fashioned parlor, Alec responded to the Reverend Schultz's questions with the reverence and sincerity of a man who was marrying the woman of his dreams. Raising her hand to his lips, he briefly kissed her fingers after slipping the diamond-encrusted wedding ring he'd purchased that afternoon onto the third finger of her left hand.

After the license had been issued at City Hall, Alec had insisted she accompany him to the town jewelry store to pick out rings. He'd ignored her suggestion that they use Band-Aids. In the shop she'd refused to voice any opinion whatsoever, seeing the sparkling gold-and-diamond jewelry as miniature handcuffs intended only as a psychological reminder that she would be shackled to the obstinate man for a year. Less, if she had her way about it, but even one day would be too much.

To the few well-wishers Leona had invited, his gesture probably appeared to be genuine. What would her friends say if they knew the truth? That this man planned not only to destroy her ranch land, but possibly bring about such catastrophic change it would send a tidal wave well beyond her borders and affect the lives of everyone standing in this room. She felt like a traitor hiding it from them. But Leona had agreed that to tell anyone the truth would only create unnecessary worry and add pressure on Shea she didn't need. Her sole focus had to be on the war against this man. And *when* she won, no one would ever be the wiser.

Consequently, Alec Morreston had been introduced as the long lost love she'd met while at college. Family concerns had taken him away but now he was back in her life and neither wanted to wait a second longer to marry. Shea could tell Alec had fought not to laugh when she'd told him the plan, but he'd agreed to it. And why not? He wouldn't be around to explain if this whole thing blew up in her face. She hoped she'd make it through this night without being sick.

"Do you, Shea Elizabeth Hardin, take this man to be your lawfully wedded husband…?"

As she reluctantly, obligingly recited her promise to love, honor and obey the irritating man, she glanced once in his direction and couldn't mistake the pursing of his lips as he fought to suppress a wicked smile from spreading across his face. She gritted her teeth as she shoved the gold wedding band onto his finger, not daring to look at him again. She wasn't near the actress she needed to be to pull off a convincing smile.

"By the authority vested in me, I now pronounce you husband and wife." The Reverend Schultz smiled at her before turning to Alec. "You may kiss your bride."

Reality became surreal as she looked at Alec, this stranger, who was now legally her husband. She had only seconds to comprehend the full impact of what she'd done before he pulled her into his arms and raised her face to meet his.

"Too late for any regrets, Mrs. Morreston," he whispered, as if reading her mind. He lowered his head and his mouth covered hers.

Like a bolt of electric current, something exploded within, causing her senses to whirl and the room to spin. She grabbed the lapels of his suit in an effort to steady herself.

With practiced skill, he parted her lips and his tongue entered the deeper recesses of her mouth. His hand cupped the back of her head, holding her to him, as he filled her mouth with his raw, male flavor. Despite her resolve to remain impervious to this man and unaffected by his touch, she found herself responding to the sensuous temptations he offered.

Her hand left his shoulder to touch the texture of his face, letting her fingertips glide along the strong line of his jaw until finally coming to rest at the point where his mouth joined with hers.

Then he withdrew from her and she couldn't deny a slight feeling of disappointment. With his thumb, he gently wiped the moisture from her lips as he studied her expression. A frown drew his dark brows together and he searched her face as if seeking an answer to a silent question. Had he been as affected by the kiss as she had?

Then a slow, sexy grin spread across his features and a knowing gleam flashed in the golden depths of his eyes before he stepped to her side to receive the offers of congratulations from the small group of people who stood smiling around them. She inhaled deeply, frustrated at her own momentary weakness.

Somehow, she managed to be pleasant as she introduced her new husband to her closest friends and neighbors, all the while praying they would never find out what was at stake beneath the façade of this marriage. The last thing she needed was concerned neighbors who feared for their own livelihood distracting her from her primary objective of getting rid of the man.

The photographer Leona had arranged through the local newspaper began to position them for their wedding photos. Someone made an off-color comment about the wedding night. Everyone joined in the banter and laughter abounded, but it only served to drive home the depravity of her situation.

A chill settled over her. What kind of man was Alec Morreston? Would he be understanding of her feelings or completely insensitive? She couldn't stop her eyes from straying to this man who potentially held the future of the ranch, as well as her own well-being, in his hands.

Alec glanced at his new bride. Immediately he noted the anxiety that was obvious in every delicate feature of her face, and he didn't have to be hit over the head to know the cause. His laughter faded as he recognized the depth of her apprehension. She was frightened.

Of him.

The fact should have made him happy. It was the first step toward making her leave. Such quick success should be sweet. So why did he feel sickened by her fear?

Their eyes met. The glistening blue of hers held him transfixed. Somewhere a light flashed, the brilliance challenging the intensity of the moment, capturing it forever.

Then, she seemed to gather her reserves and in a barely perceived movement, she straightened her shoulders and raised her chin. The near panic and vulnerability he'd caught a glimpse of moments before were now replaced with a look of pride and stubborn determination. With sudden insight, Alec knew that while he'd often admired beauty in other women, never had he appreciated their character or inner strength.

"Good one," he heard someone say. "Now if you'll both turn this way…and let's see some smiles!"

With the speed and brilliance of the camera's flash, Alec knew he was in trouble. He swallowed hard. While admittedly attracted to her, he'd previously ignored the sparks that ignited between them whenever their eyes found each other. He'd told himself he looked at all women the way he looked at Shea Harden. He'd just never noticed before.

He'd lied to himself.

He'd never been smitten by any woman. Whatever he'd felt for Sondra in the beginning was not even close to this. And the soft blush on Shea's face when she'd caught him staring told him the attraction was not one-sided.

There was definitely something between them. Like a force field of pure energy, it surrounded them. The air crackled every time they got close to each other. Where this put him in the overall scheme of things, he wasn't sure. He knew an affair would only complicate matters, but the temptation to throw caution to the wind was overwhelming.

As Shea closed the front door behind the last of the departing guests, she realized that for a few crazy minutes she'd actually forgotten about Alec. Reaching over to pick up a wineglass left on a nearby table, she took several steps toward the kitchen before she noticed him.

Leaning against the newel post at the foot of the stairs with his arms crossed casually in front of him, he had discarded his tie and unbuttoned his white dress shirt at the neck. The long sleeves were rolled up midarm and Shea noticed a gold watch nestled amid the sprinkling of dark hair on his tanned wrist. She also caught the dull gleam of the gold wedding band. The color drained from her face.

She clenched and unclenched her hands around the stemware as something close to panic settled into every inch of her body. She raised her chin in an effort to appear nonchalant as she crossed the room and entered the kitchen. Alec followed. Stepping up behind her, he reached around and removed the wineglass from the death grip she had on it, placing it on the counter next to the sink. The shrill ring of the telephone was a welcome intrusion. She hurried across the room and grabbed it on the second ring.

"I hear you've been looking for me," said a male voice. "It's about time!"

"David?" No. No. No. This could not be happening. Not now.

"Who else?" His voice was as jovial as she remembered. "How the hell are you, Shea?"

"I…I'm good. It's so good to hear your voice." *Understatement. Exclamation mark.*

"Right back at ya, Doc." The nickname he'd always used while she studied to be a veterinarian caused her heart to swell. She could sense him grinning. "So, I got a call from Marcy Allen. She said you've been trying to reach me. What can I do?"

Marry me, she wanted to scream. She closed her eyes as the irony washed over her. Why couldn't he have called yesterday? Or even this morning.

"Ah. Well…actually it's nothing. I mean, the problem has been resolved."

"Are you sure?"

Shea chanced a look in Alec's direction. Was that a smirk on his face?

"Yeah. I'm sure." At least as far as David was concerned. It was just after midnight and the bizarre marriage to Alec Morreston was in full swing. *Her* problem was just beginning.

They spoke for a few more minutes, then with a promise to keep in touch, they said goodbye. And just like that, the positive energy holding the tension at bay seemed to evaporate from the room.

"Old boyfriend?" Alec asked quietly.

She nodded.

"Gee. That's too bad. One day too late." He didn't sound a bit sorry as she crossed the room, returning to the sink, not certain what her next move should be. Alec followed and slowly slid his arms around her waist. His face rubbed against her hair, the heat from his body warm against her back.

"I like your friends that were here tonight," he murmured near her ear. His breath was hot against her neck. In such close proximity, his deep voice caused tingling sensations to dance over her skin. Shea clung to the edge of the counter for support.

She tried to remain calm. "They are good people."

"It was nice of them to come on such short notice."

"Yes. Leona…called most of them."

He stepped away and she heard the clink of ice. Glancing over her shoulder, she watched as Alec pulled a partially consumed bottle of champagne from its silver canister. Holding two crystal flutes easily in one hand, he poured the champagne with the other.

"To what shall we toast?" he asked as he handed her one of the glasses. "A long and satisfying marriage?"

She eyed him coolly. "How about to integrity?"

He pursed his lips as if to contain a devilish grin, then tipped his head and touched his fluted glass to hers. She downed the full contents, desperately needing the champagne's calming effect. She rarely drank alcohol, never champagne, and she wasn't prepared for the sensation. Her eyes clouded with tears and she couldn't stop the choking cough.

Still, the night that lay ahead made her hold the empty glass out to Alec. She ignored the knowing smile tugging at the corners of his mouth as he obligingly refilled it to the brim.

If it were within her power to disappear in a puff of smoke, she'd have done it. For one fleeting second the land didn't seem *that* important. Then the moment passed and she knew she'd see this thing through.

Somehow.

"It's been a long day," he said when she set her empty glass on the table.

"Yes." She readily agreed, some hope suddenly flaring in her chest.

"I suggest you show me our room."

Alec ignored any traces of panic that must have been apparent in her face and, without waiting for an answer, reached for her hand. His was large and warm, his grip firm and solid as he led her out of the kitchen and toward the stairs, turning off the lights as he went.

Lifting the long skirt of the gown with her free hand to ensure she didn't step on the hem, she followed him up the stairs. At the top of the staircase, he paused, silently indicating she should precede him into a bedroom. She walked down the hall, her head held high.

At the door to her room, she stopped. *I can't do this.* She felt light-headed. She could almost hear the chaotic beating of her heart as it pounded against her ribs.

Reaching around her, Alec turned the knob and effortlessly pushed open the door. She hesitated, swallowing back the vile taste of fear that rose in her throat. She could feel the warmth of his body against her back and the soft caress of his breath on her ear seconds before he kissed the sensitive area just below. Wild sensations tore through her. She spun around to face him, her hands braced against the muscled wall of his chest as she tried to keep him at arm's length.

"What's the matter?" he asked, tilting his head in mock innocence. "Wedding night jitters?"

"No." She shook her head. "No. It's just that…well, we…

we don't know each other. I mean…" She took a step back from him, placing her just inside the bedroom.

"I think I know a way we can remedy that problem." He began to unbutton his shirt. With his other hand, he reached out and flipped off the bedroom light leaving only the soft beams of moonlight that streamed through the window to challenge the darkness that now surrounded them. In the dim glow, he watched her, his gaze focused on her lips.

Shea slowly backed away but Alec advanced toward her, matching her step for step. With the last button released, his shirt fell open to reveal the muscular wall of his chest. She hadn't realized he was so powerfully built; so solid. Definitely not the body of a man who sat behind a desk every day.

"You surprise me, Mrs. Morreston. I had expected you to come down the stairs wearing boots and jeans. Instead, you walked into the room in that gown." The deep, velvety texture of his voice made her shiver. "If that was for my benefit, to ensure I knew what a beautiful and desirable woman I was about to marry, you can rest assured, it worked."

"It…it was my mother's."

"It's very nice. Very elegant." He continued to advance toward her. "But now it's time to take it off."

"No."

"No?" He mocked her. "Why, Mrs. Morreston, are you saying you intend to deny your husband on our wedding night?"

"I…I just think we need time to—"

"Don't worry, sweetheart," he cut in. "We have all night, and I certainly intend to take my time."

"No!"

"No? Might I remind you, Mrs. Morreston, you're now a very wealthy woman. You played a good hand and put me in a position of having to marry you in order to keep my own land. Almost diabolical when you think about it. But all the benefits don't swing in one direction. It's now my turn to see what I get in exchange for giving up my freedom."

"No."

"There's that word again." Alec didn't bother concealing his devious smile. "Are you saying you want to have our marriage annulled and give up so soon? I honestly believed your resolve to keep this place, no matter what, would last longer than the wedding night."

"And I hoped, as a gentleman, you would afford me an opportunity to get to know you before…before…"

"Who ever said I was a gentleman?" Shea could see the faint white of his teeth as he smiled in the darkness. "I've held up my end of this bargain, Mrs. Morreston. Now, I believe, it's your turn."

"Stop calling me that!" she snapped through gritted teeth as her inner turmoil exploded to the surface. This only succeeded in causing a bigger grin to spread across his face.

"But that's who you are, *Mrs. Morreston*." His fingers reached out and touched the tiny pearl buttons at the neckline of her dress. "It was your decision, remember?"

"Only to prevent you from taking my ranch."

"It was your decision."

Shea swallowed back the alarm that threatened to engulf her. He was right. He had warned her. And she had agreed freely.

Reaching for one of her hands, he began to unbutton the seam that ran from her wrist to her elbow, letting the satiny material fall away from her arm. Then, without a word, he moved to the other sleeve.

That completed, in a gentle but firm action, he turned her around and began to unfasten the back of the satin-and-lace gown. His hands moved slowly, methodically down the dress, releasing button after tiny button.

She caught their reflection in the mirror on the closet

door. The moonlight highlighted the silver-blond strands of her hair and softened the panicked features of her face. Alec's large, dark silhouette loomed behind her, his head bowed as he worked at his task. All traces of his earlier amusement were gone, replaced by a look of serious intent.

Standing practically nude before a strange man was not an experience she'd ever anticipated. The gown provided a frail armor, a subtle safeguard. In a few precious minutes, her lace panties and the white hosiery would be the only pieces of armor that remained.

Their eyes met in the mirror for countless seconds before he bent his head and placed his lips against the sensitive area beneath her ear. Her heart kicked into double time as Alec emitted a low growl, which sent electric sensations racing down her spine.

She spun around in an effort to break the contact. Rather than reach for her again, he removed his shirt, tossed it aside and began unbuckling his belt. The muscles of his shoulders and arms rippled in the moon's glow, the significant pectorals making him seem even bigger than he'd looked with his clothes on.

Taking another step back from him, her legs bumped against the bed. Her pulse tripled. Frantically her eyes searched the room, hoping to detect any means of escape from this reprehensible situation.

Before she could voice any more objections or seize on a reason to try to postpone the inevitable, Alec reached out to her. His hands cupped her face, compelling her to meet his gaze as he took the final step, closing the short distance between them.

Shea clenched her hands into tight fists at her sides, determined to resist this forceful male. In the pale light, she saw his eyes focus on her lips seconds before his mouth came down over hers hard, masterfully firm in its possession. His hands left her face as his heavy arms encircled her body like bands of steel. His sheer strength and size, coupled with the passion of the embrace, rocked her senses and snatched the very breath from her lungs. She was way out of her depth. A feeling of near hysteria enveloped her mind. With a small cry, she tore her mouth from his. He allowed her to pull back but kept her close, his large hands resting on her shoulders.

"I can't...I can't do this." Her fingers gripped his. "I know you said...I know I agreed that...but I...please... don't—"

"Shh." A frown drew his dark brows together. He had to see the frantic, almost terrified expression that must be on her face, mirroring the fear churning inside. "It's all right, Shea. I'm not going to hurt you," he murmured as his thumbs caressed the side of her face. "Just kiss me. That's all you have to do."

Shea scarcely had time to nod her agreement before his mouth once again claimed hers. This time he moved slowly, sensuously, with an easy gentleness that immediately began to tear down the walls of her resistance. His tongue licked and teased her lips, moistening them, as if readying her for a more intense joining.

With consummate skill, he encouraged her lips to open. His tongue slid deep into the cavern of her mouth, sending her heart plummeting all the way to her knees. The kiss was frankly intimate, shamefully enticing and custom designed to evoke a matching response from her. He tasted of champagne and his own uniquely delicious male flavor. It mingled with the bittersweet essence of his cologne, which silently affirmed the raw masculinity of the man who wore it.

His hands rubbed her back, working down her spine, slowly massaging away the last remnants of her inner turmoil. Sensual warmth began to spread though her, intensifying the heat pooling between her legs while a thread of confusion wove its way into her mind.

What am I doing? But the question was too fleeting to receive an answer.

Slowly but steadily, her fear began to change form, turning instead into a fundamental need that refused to be ignored. A fragment of her mind insisted this wasn't right. Her body screamed that it was.

Alec pushed the creamy fabric of the gown from her shoulders. It fell to the floor with a quiet rustle. She should have been shocked, but the realization weighed no heavier than the soft evening breeze entering the room through the open windows. For a few moments in time, she forgot the reality of her situation, of her pledged hatred of this man. Of their own accord, her arms slid up over his muscled chest to rest on his broad, powerful shoulders, letting her fingers play in the thick, silky texture of his hair. Alec's hands moved lower in their rotation until, reaching the fullness of her hips, he pulled her firmly up and against him. The hard, male ridge of his arousal pressed against the sensitive juncture between her legs and a jolt of pure sexual hunger shot through her. Her body jerked forward, uncontrollably, bringing a deep growl from Alec.

He began to alternately kiss and nibble the delicate contours of her neck and shoulder and, eyes closed, she tilted her head to allow him greater access. His hands moved to her breasts, kneading the firmness, making them swell under his touch. Then his mouth returned to hers in a deep, drugging kiss that brought a small whimper, an automatic response conveying the end of her struggle against the inevitable.

Five

Experience told Alec that sound signified her acceptance of what was to come. He knew, at this moment in time she was his, completely and totally. Raising his head, he looked at Shea's face, radiant in the moonlight. Her eyes were closed, her lips parted as if waiting for his mouth to return. As if beckoning his lips to return.

Heat coursed through his body, centering in his loins, making him throb against the restricting barrier of his slacks. A slight tremor reminded him he was about to cross the line. This was not the plan. Seducing her wouldn't accomplish anything except add to the problems he already faced and enormously complicate the entire situation.

He gritted his teeth, closed his eyes and fought for restraint. But even when he couldn't see, her fragrance assailed him, called to him and tempted him almost beyond his control. He knew her body craved fulfillment and her need only served to bring him closer to that moment of ultimate possession, a moment that should never happen. He ached with wanting. His libido screamed, *Take her*!

Suddenly, it was too much.

Damn the land. Damn that contract. Damn this situation. With a groan of defeat, he scooped her into his arms, laid her gently on the bed and followed her down, his mouth again finding hers.

Then, almost unnoticeable at first, a persistent sound of drumming broke into the moment. The sound, hesitant but determined, brought with it a cold reality that refused to leave.

Frowning, Alec raised his head, reluctantly separating his lips from hers. He inhaled deeply, fighting to regain cognizant thought. It sounded as if someone was knocking on a door. Silence. Then it started again. Another hard series of raps caused him to look questioningly at Shea while he fought to latch onto some thread of reality.

"Are you expecting anyone?" His voice sounded rough, even to his own ears.

She mutely looked into his face. Alec drew a deep breath and blew it out, pausing to regain what little mind he had left. Finally, he rolled off the bed and stood up. Taking another deep breath, he walked out into the hallway and down the stairs as the persistent knocking continued. He knew a sudden surge of fury as he reached the kitchen door.

Hank Minton, the ranch foreman, stood on the doorstep. He had his hat in his hands, and a worried look pinched the strained features of his face. He wouldn't look Alec in the eye. Instead he watched the bugs fluttering around the porch light, studied the doorbell and finally appeared to give significant attention to his old, worn boots.

"Hank." Suspicion set off a flashing red light in Alec's still-muddled brain.

"I'm sorry to bother you all with this," the old cowboy said. "Real sorry. Specially knowing it's your weddin' night and all. But we got a horse down and I think Shea's gonna need to take a look at him."

"I see," Alec replied. And he did.

There was no question in his mind that Shea had solicited Hank's help for this perfectly timed interruption. Alec was torn between a desire to toss the old man off the step or hug his neck and thank him for doing what Alec apparently lacked the strength to do himself.

Hank had just provided a plausible excuse for Alec to

stop, which was exactly what *he* should have done in the first place. Annoyance surged through him for his weakness and for letting his desire overcome his common sense.

He definitely should be grateful to Hank. Why, then, did he have the urge to break the old man's neck?

"Come in. I'll get her."

The old cowboy nodded and stepped just inside the kitchen, glancing at the sink, the overhead light, the chairs and finally back to his boots.

Shea sat on the edge of the bed in the darkened room as reality came slamming back. Willing her pulse to steady, she took a deep breath in a desperate attempt to clear her head. Her hand trembled as she ran her fingers through her hair. It had been close. Too close. His touch left the lower parts of her body swollen, unfulfilled and badly in need of something more.

He hadn't made love to her. Technically. Hadn't penetrated her body with his. She should be monumentally happy. Why, then, did she feel ridiculously disappointed?

She stood and felt her way to the closet, not bothering to turn on a light. Her legs were strangely weak. She quickly shucked her hosiery, pulled on a pair of jeans and a shirt and then descended the stairs. She couldn't help but grimace as the full impact of the situation settled over her.

She'd almost had sex with Alec Morreston.

Even worse, he hadn't forced her. He hadn't held her down or tied her to the bedposts. He'd kissed her. That was all. Apparently, that had been enough. She knew it. And worse, so did he. Alec was here to take away her ranch, her home, everything she held dear. She would do well to remember that. He was, inarguably, a very potent package with obvious experience to back that up. She had to be strong.

Alec pivoted from the open doorway as she entered the

kitchen. He didn't appear surprised to see her there. "It seems your presence is needed in the barn." His tone clearly said he was suspicious of Hank's timing.

"It's Crusty, Shea." Hank's voice carried to her from the doorway. "He's down. Me and Jason, we've been working with him almost an hour, but we can't keep him on his feet. I think it's colic." The old cowboy threaded the brim of his hat through his hands in a nervous gesture as he stared at his boots. "I'm real sorry about this. Real sorry."

"That's okay, Hank." Shea glanced at Alec. "I'm sure Mr. Morreston understands." The look Alec gave her clearly said he understood far more than just the claimed need for Shea's presence in the barn. "Give me a second to put on some shoes. Is he in the main barn?"

"Yes, ma'am. I'll go on back out there." He put his hat firmly on his head and turned toward the door. "I'm real sorry 'bout this. Real sorry." Hank closed the door behind him.

Shea ran up the stairs and into the bedroom, wasting no time as she pulled on socks and boots. Just as she stood and reached for her jacket, Alec walked into the room.

"Need any help?"

"No. Thanks anyway."

As she walked past him, he gently touched her shoulder, stopping her in midstride.

"Consider this…a wedding gift. We wouldn't want all of Hank's efforts to be for nothing. But, take fair warning, next time there will be no interruptions. You can accept that or you can prepare to leave here." There was a gleam of promise in his eyes.

His insolence was like a splash of cold water. A scant few minutes ago, she'd been on the verge of giving herself to this man. Now her only inclination was to put her fist firmly against his nose with the highest velocity she could muster. The combined emotions of frustration and humiliation propelled her anger to the surface.

Pushing past him, she almost ran down the stairs.

When she pulled open the heavy barn door, she found Hank holding the lead shank attached to a halter placed on one of the older geldings.

"Figured he might come with you," Hank explained. "Ole Crusty here looks like he just might keel over any minute. A city feller wouldn't know the difference." Shea smiled and nodded. "Was I convincin'? Did I do okay?"

"Yeah." She nodded her approval as she walked toward the old horse. "You did good, Hank."

Her plan had worked. The timing could have been a little better, but even so, good enough. So why wasn't she bouncing-off-the-walls deliriously happy? Why did she feel so incomplete? In all honesty, she had to admit deep down a part of her regretted the interruption.

Alec knew a woman's body. He knew exactly where to touch, precisely how to kiss and just what to do to make a female respond to him. To make *her* respond to him. From the beginning, she'd sensed he would be highly skilled in bed, but she'd never envisioned finding out firsthand. She could still taste him, could feel his hard body against hers. His masculine scent was heavy on her skin. The fire he'd lit still burned, refusing to die out. Taking a deep, shaky breath, she sat down on a bale of hay and rubbed her forehead in an attempt to clear her mind. But the remembrance of what had happened—of what had almost happened—stubbornly wouldn't go away.

"Missy, are you sure you know what you're doing?" Hank removed his hat and scratched his head, which left his thinning gray hair in a tousled mess on top of his head, then replaced his timeworn hat.

"Absolutely." She smiled bravely, confidently at the old cowboy. But she knew she was lying through her teeth.

* * *

Alec watched as Shea almost ran down the stairs. He raked his hand through his hair and took a deep breath. It had been too close. Three minutes, maybe less, and their bodies would have been locked in the most intimate act that could happen between two people and nothing on this earth would have made him let her go. He wasn't exactly sure how he'd allowed the situation to escalate as far as it had and he wasn't certain how to prevent it in the future.

The plan had been to frighten her with an overload of sexual intimidation, come on so hard and heavy that she'd run like a scared rabbit. But instead of running, instead of saying, *Okay, you win, I'll leave,* she had looked up at him with those damned amazing blue eyes and silently begged him not to hurt her, pleaded with him to give her time. And in that instant, with her enticing lips a mere breath away, and those eyes imploring him to understand, he'd made a choice. And that choice had almost irrevocably changed everything.

He couldn't remember ever losing control or being blindsided by the aura of a sexy woman. But this time his strength of will had flown out the window and he'd almost sacrificed everything for a young woman from the back woods of Texas with big blue eyes and one hell of a game plan. So much for his ironclad resolve.

He had to get out of here, at least for a while. Let things cool down and give himself time to regain his perspective, to reformulate his plan. With a grimace, he turned and walked toward the bathroom and a cold shower.

The sun was just peeking over the distant hills when Shea quietly made her way back to the house. The romantics of the world could say all they wanted about sleeping on a soft bed of hay. In truth, it was prickly and itchy and its stiff, needlelike projections could poke through even the thickest blanket right into your skin. She hadn't had a good night. But the few hours of restless sleep had been enough to restore her sanity. In the light of day, she knew the outcome of the previous night could have been much worse.

She could have made love to Alec.

She could be lying in that bed right now with his big, muscled arms securely around her, drowsy in the aftermath of their lovemaking. Feeling— *Stop!* With a muttered oath, Shea pulled open the back door.

When she entered the kitchen, to her surprise, Alec was already there dressed in dark slacks, a clean white dress shirt and tie. He looked disgustingly well-rested.

"Looks like you had a good night," he said, reaching out to pull some straw from her tangled hair. "You give an entirely new meaning to a roll in the hay. Sleep well, did you?" His mouth twitched in amusement as he gestured to the pot of fresh coffee.

Shea ignored his jibes, opened the cabinet and selected a mug. If he expected her to make any comment about what happened last night—or what *hadn't* happened—he could hold his breath until he turned blue.

She couldn't help noticing the way his shirt did little to hide the muscles of his arm as he lifted his cup to his mouth, or the way his full lips opened against the rounded edge of the mug as he sipped the steaming coffee. She quickly turned away as unsettling sensations began to send surges of heat through her veins.

"I need to return home for a few days," Alec said as she reached for the coffee. "I understand this might be viewed as deserting my wife on our honeymoon, but I'm afraid it can't be helped. As far as the contract, I don't recall any stipulation that I never leave the boundaries of the land, only that I ensure your protection from *any and all perils*. If you think you'll be *safe* for a few days—" his sarcasm was apparent "—I need clothes. And I need to make some arrangements. Do our attorneys need to become involved with this?"

In spite of the temptation to try to deny Alec the time he needed, she knew it wouldn't be right. And there was nothing in the contract to prevent him from leaving the property.

"No. But I wouldn't bother packing a lot of clothes. You won't be here long enough to need them."

At least his trip would give her the time she needed to form a better plan to make him leave permanently. With any luck, he wouldn't come back at all.

He watched her guardedly. "Want to come with me?"

"No, thank you," she quickly responded. "I've got things I need to see to here."

"I'm sure you do," he replied, tongue in cheek. "How's the horse?"

"The horse?" she frowned. It took a few seconds before she remembered the "sick" horse in the barn. "Oh. Fine. Good." She looked down at her mug and away from the scrutiny of those amber eyes, knowing she was incapable of telling a convincing lie. "I expect he'll make a full recovery."

"Oh, I have no doubt."

Alec walked to the counter where she stood and reached around her to place his cup in the sink. "Call a local furniture store and have them send out a larger bed. Get an entire suite if you like."

The surprise must have shown on her face.

"Is money a problem?"

"No." She shook her head. "But a larger bed won't fit into that room."

"Then have it put in a larger room." He cocked his head. "There *is* a larger bedroom, isn't there?"

"Yes, but…"

Alec watched her reaction. "But what?"

There were in fact three bedrooms upstairs. But moving

into the master indicated a permanency she did not want. She just wished he would stay wherever it was he was going and let her life return to normal.

"Nothing." She shook her head. "How long will you be away?" She didn't want to ask. To do so might imply she cared. But she had to prepare for his return.

"A few days. Possibly a week. I can't be sure. Why? Will you miss me?"

She snorted and took a sip of her coffee.

"I'll take that as a yes."

He tucked a loose strand of hair behind her ear before his head dipped toward her and his lips found hers. It was instinct rather than conscious thought that made her open to him. He deepened the embrace, kissing her thoroughly but briefly. Then, raising his head, he broke the contact but remained close.

"You're going to lose," Alec whispered. "But this challenge is becoming more interesting by the minute. I look forward to the next round."

Her expression strengthened into a cold glare. But before she could respond in kind, he turned and walked out the door.

The large private jet sliced through the white clouds en route back to Dallas from New York LaGuardia. After a week of reflection, Alec was no closer to finding a concrete plan that would ensure he maintained control of the bizarre situation.

So far, the only thing guaranteed to work was avoiding her altogether. But not only would that not serve his objective, it was not something he was willing to do.

He glanced at the child, asleep on the small bed across the aisle. This morning, when he'd picked up his bag and prepared to leave for the airport, he'd seen Scotty peeking around the corner of the kitchen doorway. He'd walked over to his son, lifted the four-year-old into his arms and given in to the overwhelming need to hold him close.

"Are you gonna be gone a long time?"

Alec had given him a regretful smile. "Maybe not too long this time."

"Good. Where are you going?"

"Actually, I'll be staying on a ranch."

"A ranch?"

"Yep."

"Do they have horsees?"

"I believe they do."

"And cowboys?" Scotty's eyes had been wide with excitement.

"And cowboys," he'd confirmed as an idea had formed in his mind.

It had been a spur-of-the-moment decision to bring him along, but even now, some three hours later, Alec still felt it was the right one. Scott's preschool was over for the summer. Alec spent far too much time away from his son because of the requirements of his work. This wacky situation actually might provide some time to spend with his son, an experience both he and Scotty would remember.

The only negative he could see was the possibility Shea and Scott might bond, which could be tough on the boy when it was time to leave. It was because of this concern Alec elected to not mention the marriage. To tell Scotty he had a mother only to take him away from her a couple of weeks later was just wrong. He wouldn't do that to Scott.

Alec's mouth quirked as he thought of Shea and the days ahead. As far as he knew, Shea had no children and possibly no experience with a four-year-old. This unexpected twist could prove very interesting.

He rose from his seat and entered the area of the plane set up as his office. They were still an hour out from DFW. He might as well get some work done while he could. He

had a feeling his time away from the ranch had provided
Shea with ample opportunity to put some plans in motion
to try to make him give up and leave.

Good luck with that.

"Okay, that should do her," Shea said, removing the rub-
ber surgical gloves and giving the mare's shoulder a pat.
"Take her back to the stall and keep an eye on her."

"Sure thing, boss." Hank picked up his hat and slapped
it against his leg to dislodge some of the dirt before fitting
it firmly onto his head.

The mare carried one of the best bloodlines in a five-
state region. It was the boost this ranch needed. That was
the only reason Shea tolerated Bonnie Blue's ridiculous
temperament every time the mare needed medical care.
Thankfully, it didn't happen often.

With three cowboys holding the high-strung horse, Shea
had still been thrown hard against the side of the barn when
she'd attempted to inject a tranquilizer. Her shoulder had
absorbed most of the impact, providing a painful souvenir
she would no doubt carry for a few days. Once the tranquilizer had begun to take effect, it took no time to stitch
the mare's cut, apply a topical dressing and give Bonnie
Blue the added safety of a tetanus booster.

Shea bent to pick up the discarded cotton, linens and
syringes, not bothering to watch the three lanky cowboys
lead the now docile mare out of the paddock. When she
again looked up, the breath died in her throat as she found
herself staring directly into Alec's scowling face.

He'd gone from being like a character from a foggy, half-
forgotten dream to suddenly materializing right in front of
her as a crystal clear vision. And he was as disturbingly
handsome as ever. His tall stature, the broad width of his
shoulders and the sheer male essence of him seemed even
more pronounced than she remembered.

As she approached the paddock gate, Alec swung it open and then closed it behind her.

"You want to tell me just what in the hell you were doing?"

"What do you mean?" She frowned, clueless as to what he could be talking about.

"You. That horse. You were almost killed."

Rolling her eyes, she moved to walk past him but the distinctive voice of a child abruptly shattered the tension of the moment, halting her in midstride.

"Boy, oh boy! That was *cool*!"

Shea's head snapped around in surprise. She focused on a small boy clinging precariously to the centerboard of the paddock fence, allowing the crown of his head and two large round eyes to peek over the top.

The child jumped from his perch and ran toward the gate to stand directly in front of Shea.

"Are you all right?" His small face held a look of genuine concern. "Did the horse hurt your arm?"

"No, I'm…fine." She sent a questioning glance at Alec.

"This is Scotty." He watched her face as if ready to gauge her reaction. "My son."

Shea blinked. More than twice. Alec had a child? Good Lord! Devils didn't normally produce such angelic-looking offspring, did they?

"Scotty, this is Shea."

She knew a look of disbelief covered her features as she leaned over, bringing her closer to eye-level with the boy.

"Hi, Scotty." She forced a smile and held out her hand. The boy placed his small hand in hers and produced a wide grin. Then, mysteriously struck with a bout of shyness, he stepped back to stand closer to his father, his arm around Alec's leg.

"You never told me you had a son."

Alec flexed his shoulders. "So now you know. As I was

about to leave I mentioned I would be staying on a ranch." Alec looked down at his son before returning those tawny eyes to her. "He wanted to come and see the horses and cowboys."

Are you freaking kidding me? She could only gasp as her blood pressure shot up to dangerous heights. Momentarily at a total loss for words, she forced herself to breathe deep and stared at the man standing four feet in front of her. He was insane. This child had no business on a working ranch. Not only had this conceited lunatic returned, but he'd brought an innocent child along as his backup. And she'd thought the situation couldn't possibly get any worse.

"Are you ready for the next one, Shea?" Hank asked from the side door of the main barn.

"Take a break, Hank." Her voice was unnaturally high even to her own ears.

"We need to talk." She shot an if-looks-could-kill glance at Alec and headed to the house, muttering under her breath.

Her shoulder throbbed. She longed for a nice hot soak in the tub and something to eat, but until she finished checking and treating the remaining horses, she knew she couldn't stop. The preliminary work for the annual fall roundup and branding would begin in earnest in just a few weeks. There was a great deal of preparation between now and then, and most of it rested on her shoulders. Alec couldn't have picked a worse time to return. Let alone with a child in tow.

Entering the kitchen, she tossed the dirty gauze into the trash bin before washing her hands. To give herself time to calm down she took a pitcher of tea from the refrigerator and set three glasses on the counter. Adding ice to two before filling with tea, she then poured fresh milk into the third.

"Have a seat," she told Alec, indicating the kitchen chairs when he and Scotty followed her inside. Her eyes were drawn to the child. She guessed his age to be four or five.

He was a miniature of his father except his hair was several shades lighter than Alec's dark mahogany brown.

"If you look in the big jar on the cabinet, I think you'll find some cookies."

Scotty wasted no time in pulling a chair over to the counter and climbing up to reach the cookie jar.

"Can I have two?" He flashed a smile that would melt the coldest heart. She'd bet he'd learned that from his father.

"Sure." She tried to return his smile but wasn't fully convinced she'd pulled it off. "There are some paper towels next to the sink. Grab one and your cookies and follow me. You can watch cartoons while I talk with your dad."

"I like cartoons."

With Scotty contentedly watching TV and munching on the homemade cookies in the next room, Shea returned to the kitchen and joined Alec at the table.

He'd shed his usual business suit; snug-fitting jeans now hugged his muscled thighs and a tan sports shirt hung casually from his broad shoulders. Ostrich-skin boots completed the ensemble and to her surprise, they weren't new. His tawny eyes were as compelling and enigmatic as ever.

"You said you wanted to talk?" Alec sat back in the chair looking completely at ease.

"Yeah." She set the glasses of tea on the table and dropped into a chair opposite Alec. Where to begin? What to say to a complete schmuck? "This is a working ranch. What you saw out there today happens all the time. It's what we do. This is not a pony club or a dude ranch. We don't cater to novices who don't know the nose from the back end of a horse. A child could get hurt, especially a little one who has never been around livestock. I cannot halt the operations of this ranch to play nursemaid to either one of you."

He merely looked at her, his eyes sliding from her mouth

to her breasts and back to her eyes. It was unnerving. *He* was unnerving.

"Every year we usually find at least two poisonous snakes near the main barn or around the house," she continued, determined to ignore the pulsing sensation in the pit of her stomach. "Go into the forested sections and you're likely to find cougars or bear. There are wild boars that can take a man's leg off. This is no place for a child."

"Sorry. Maybe I misunderstood. Didn't you grow up here?"

She could only glare. What could she honestly say to that?

"I will not be held responsible if an innocent little boy gets hurt."

He shrugged. "I'll have a talk with Scott. Tell me his boundaries and I'll see he stays within them."

"Then tell him to stay inside this house."

"Don't be ridiculous."

"*Me* ridiculous?"

"I have a son I love very much. I do not intend to leave him back in New York or make him stay in the house for however long it takes you to pack your bags."

Her annoyance shot across the line to pure fury at his insolence. The wooden chair made a screeching sound as she bounded to her feet. Her hands rested on the table as she leaned toward Alec. "I can't believe you'd stoop so low as to bring an innocent child into this…insanity."

Alec met her angry glare and rose slowly from his chair like a mountain lion ready to pounce. His hands rested on his side of the table as he leaned toward her. "*I* didn't cause this. *I* was not the one who refused to relinquish possession of land that didn't belong to me!"

"Oh, yes," she hissed, her voice coated with vehemence. "Just try and convince me you're the innocent victim! Do you make a habit of throwing people out of their homes?

Do you get your kicks from watching them scurry around trying to find another place to live?"

"I offered you a sizeable sum of money to leave. Not exactly the same as throwing you out on the street."

"Money. All you seem to care about is money! I feel sorry for you, Alec. I pity your son that he must live the kind of life you deem appropriate when you don't even know what family or tradition is all about."

"Leave Scotty out of this."

"*I'm* not the one who brought him into it!"

"And you've made your feelings quite clear."

"Apparently not. You're still here."

A movement out of the corner of her eye told her they had an audience. Turning toward Scotty, she pasted a smile on her face.

"The cookies were good," he said, his gaze going back and forth from his father to Shea.

"Oh. Great." *Down shift.* "I'm glad you like them. Is the cartoon over?"

"Are you and Daddy always gonna fight at each other?" He tilted his head in a manner she'd seen his father do. Guilt quickly dissolved the anger as she realized this little boy had heard their heated exchange.

"I…I don't know, sweetie," she hedged and then decided to be honest. If she and Alec didn't kill each other before this was over, it would be nothing short of a miracle. "Your dad and I, well, we have a lot of things to work out between us. There's a lot *he* doesn't understand."

The child seemed to take the answer in stride.

"Freddy Correnski said his mommy and daddy used to fight all the time. Then Freddy and his mommy moved to another house. Are Daddy and me gonna live in your house with you?"

"Uh. Well. Yes. I guess you are," she answered, trying

to force happiness into her tone. Her eyes cut to Alec as she added, "For a while."

"Cool." He walked over to stand in front of Shea. "Sometimes Daddy gets sad and I ask him why and he says he's not sad, but I know he is 'cause he just sits there in his chair and looks real tired, but he says he's not tired but he won't get up." He took a deep breath and looked at Shea. "Will you make Daddy not be sad?"

For the life of her, Shea couldn't think of an appropriate reply. Alec, apparently, had no such difficulty.

"She is going to do her best, Scott," he said as a wide grin spread across his face. The mischievous twinkle was back in his eyes.

"Good. Can I have another cookie?"

Her voice seemed to have abandoned her, so Shea merely nodded her head.

As the youngster scrambled for the cookie jar, she whispered to Alec, "You can bring a hundred kids out here. A thousand. I'm still not going to let you have this ranch."

His eyes roamed over her face. "Why don't you show us where we'll be sleeping?" he suggested, choosing to ignore her blatant declaration. "It's been a long day. I have a feeling we're going to have an early night."

Six

Shea turned and marched toward the stairs. She didn't pause until she stood just inside the doorway to a second-floor bedroom overlooking the barn and paddock area. She crossed to the window and opened the blinds, letting the sunshine in.

"I think Scotty will be comfortable in here. If you had bothered to call and let me know he was coming, I could have had the room prepared. Yolanda, the wife of one of our ranch hands, comes in twice a week and helps with the laundry and general cleaning. She should be here soon to start dinner. I'll have her change the bedding and air the room."

"This is gonna be my room?" Scotty asked in delight, oblivious to the tension still hanging heavy between the adults. "Cool!" He ran to the bed and joyfully bounced on the springy mattress before bounding to the floor and running to the large double window. "Wow! Daddy! Look at this! Is that where you keep the horsees?" He pointed a finger at the barn.

"Some of them." Shea smiled down at Alec's son.

"Can I ride one?" He looked up at her, his bright, eager eyes hopeful.

She reached out and tousled his hair. "You'll have to ask your dad."

"He'll say okay. Won't you, Daddy?" Not waiting for an answer he added, "I like it here." He turned and surveyed the room, then nodded his head as if he'd made a great decision. "Yep. This is gonna be all right."

"I assume you brought extra clothes and personal items?" Alec nodded. "I'll get Jason to help you with your suitcases. Just tell him if you want to change anything around, move the bed, whatever."

"This will be fine."

"Hey, Daddy, where is your bed?"

Shea had started out of the room. This question, however, made her pause. Clearly, Alec hadn't shared the fact he'd gotten married with his son. She couldn't pass up the chance to see how he was going to handle this one. She turned toward him, eyebrows raised, her head tilted as she waited for the answer along with Scotty.

Alec stood staring down at the small child in front of him. He rubbed a hand over his mouth, sighed, then rested his hands on his hips. "Actually, I'm going to be sleeping… in another room."

"Where?"

"I'll be bedding down with Shea."

"How come?"

Get him, Scotty!

Alec put his large hands together, cracking his knuckles as he fought to answer that one. Then his head shot up, he glanced at Shea and back to his son. "She's afraid of the dark."

"Oh."

He did not just say that. She couldn't withhold a snort of laughter, which earned her a glare of warning from Alec.

"Okaaaaay." *Your son. Your bad.* "Well, I've still got a lot of work to do this afternoon. Yolanda will start supper about six." She again looked at Scotty. "What do you like to eat?"

"Hot dogs! With ketchup."

Her lips slid into a full, easy grin and Alec had to wonder if it had the same effect on his son as it did him. Damn, she was beautiful.

"I'll see what we can do."

As she disappeared around the corner, Scotty's voice rang out. "I *like* her, Daddy."

Alec nodded. His son had just answered his unspoken question and he wasn't surprised. He'd carried the far-fetched hope that returning to the ranch would dispel his initial attraction to Shea and he could chalk up the whole thing to stress.

No such luck.

He looked around the room. The wallpaper was faded, its edges peeling away from the walls in a couple of places. Slightly discolored stains on the ceiling indicated water had entered uninvited at some time in the past and left its murky calling card. The light fixture, a remnant from a bygone era, dangled precariously from the twelve-foot-high ceiling. The faint scents of mothballs and lemon touched his senses. But in spite of its worn appearance, this room, in fact the entire house, brought to mind childhood memories of home-baked bread and leftover meatloaf sandwiches. Of the big tree that had been outside his window, perfect for sneaking out of the house to go night fishing with Grandpa Jacob and old man Muldoon.

Alec moved to stand beside his son at the large window. Shea came into view directly below, walking toward the barn.

"Hey, Dad? Do you think she likes us?"

"Oh, I'm sure she does, son," he lied.

Shea was standing next to a big Appaloosa and a portable medic unit writing something on a form attached to a clipboard when Alec and Scotty walked into the paddock area near the main barn. The tension in her carriage was obvious. He was tempted to step over and give her shoulders a quick massage, but immediately decided against it. The last thing he needed was to get so close to temptation.

"What are you gonna do?" Scotty asked her, his eyes wide and curious.

"I gave him a shot that'll help keep him healthy," she explained simply. She patted the horse's shoulder. "Okay, Jason, take him away."

After making some additional notations she turned her attention back to Scotty. "Have you ever seen a horse get shoes?"

Scotty shook his head.

"No? Then, come with me."

Alec followed as they walked to the north end of the barn where a blacksmith had set up his rig for shoeing horses. The clang of his hammer rang out through the late afternoon calm. Alec stood slightly to the side, content to watch the interaction between Shea and his son. It appeared they already were bonding, a fact that both surprised and intrigued him.

"This is Charlie." She nodded toward the burly man dressed in a sleeveless shirt and jeans. A faded red bandana tied around his forehead kept the sweat from his eyes.

"What's he doing?"

"He's making a shoe for one of the horses." Smiling at Scotty, she selected a metal horseshoe from the trailer, handed it to him. Scotty held it as though it were made of gold.

"Each horse has different size feet, just like people do. Charlie selects a shoe close to the size of a horse's hoof, then heats the metal so when he beats it with the hammer it will change the shape a little bit until it fits. Then he cools it and nails it on."

"Doesn't it hurt?"

"Nope. He uses special nails. The horse can't feel a thing."

Scotty looked again at the metal shoe, then held it out to Shea.

"Keep it," she said. "Hang it on a wall in your room. Like this." She turned the metal shoe around so that it formed the shape of a cup. "It will catch good luck." Fascinated, Scotty smiled up at her. He took a few steps in Charlie's direction before stopping and looking back at Shea and his father.

"It's okay, son." Alec assured him. "You can go over and talk to Charlie. Just don't get too close to the horses."

He hesitated only a few seconds before walking over, proudly holding his horseshoe with both hands.

Alec was moved by the gentleness and attention she'd shown Scotty. It was something he hadn't anticipated. There was no hidden agenda he could see. Unlike some women, she certainly wasn't doing it to impress him. She seemed genuine, as though she not only enjoyed teaching Scott about the things in her world, but she honestly liked Scotty, as well. And his son seemed equally fond of her.

She glanced at Alec as she walked past to return to the medic unit.

"Thanks," he felt obliged to say.

She frowned. "For what?"

"For taking the time for Scotty."

She shrugged it off. "I like kids. He's a sweetie. There's no point in making him feel unwelcome. But you brought him. He's your son. Your responsibility. If he gets hurt, it's on you."

With that, she picked up the clipboard and began to check her data.

"How many cattle do you have?" Alec asked, glancing beyond the barn at the distant hills.

"On average the Bar H runs about three thousand head." She turned to him, her captivating eyes moving over his face. "The number, of course, drops after we ship in the fall, but is reestablished the first of the year when the calving begins."

"Shea?" Hank called from the doorway. "Where do you want Shonie?" He led a large painted gelding into the area.

"Bring him over here," Shea instructed, setting the clipboard aside.

"Is there something I can do to help?" Alec wanted something to keep his mind occupied, his hands busy. In the short time he'd been back, his body already had begun responding to her.

His question appeared to take Shea by surprise. "Have you ever been around horses?"

"Some."

"I've got eight more to check." She looked down the hallway. "The stalls are numbered. I'll need to see the ones in eight, twelve and fifteen next. Their halters, with leads attached, are hanging on the doors."

Finding the correct stall, Alec slipped the halter over the head of a docile mare and led her out of the barn.

Shea took the lead from his hands. "She's no problem. I can handle her by myself. While I check her out, go ahead and get Ransom. Number twelve."

She was just finishing with the mare when Alec arrived with the spirited bay gelding. The feisty animal nickered playfully and attempted to rub his head against Alec's shoulder.

"You seem to have made a friend."

"You sound surprised," he noted, turning to rub the neck of the striking animal. He appreciated quality and this big gelding reeked of good breeding, as did most of the horses he'd seen here.

"I am. Hold him here while I take Essie to Charlie. Her shoes need replacing."

* * *

On the horizon, fiery remnants of red and gold accented the darkening sky as Shea checked the last of the horses. When she brought the final one around the corner of the barn, she was surprised to see Scotty perched on top of one of the trail horses tied securely to the fence. Frowning, she looked at Alec, who stood next to the child.

"He's fine." Alec assured her, as though reading her mind. "Having the time of his life." His booted foot was propped on the lower rail of the fence, his jeans hugging his muscular legs and hips. His arms rested easily on the top rail. He looked lean and strong. She swallowed hard, fighting back the insane desire to walk over and step into his arms.

"I'm beat." She could hear the tiredness in her own voice, no doubt the cause of her temporary insanity. "I'll see you back at the house."

Alec nodded before she turned and headed toward the house. She refused to let her mind dwell on the night ahead and the possibilities it could hold. Entering through the kitchen door, she walked to the stairs and made it as far as the second-floor landing when she saw the open door at the end of the hall.

The master bedroom.

She stopped in her tracks.

The new furniture had been delivered, the bed prepared with clean linens and the door closed. It had remained closed—until today. Until Alec returned and opened it. Now it taunted her, dared her to enter and face the moment of truth.

She clenched her hands at her sides, fighting her growing panic. She turned and almost flew down the stairs.

Alec and Scotty were just coming in the door when Shea reached the kitchen. She grabbed her car keys and a manila folder containing information Leona had asked for a month ago.

"I'll be back," she muttered.

"Mind if I ask where you're going?"

"Um…I've got to take some records over to Leona."

Without waiting for any further comment, she quickly walked out the door.

The house was quiet when Shea stepped into the kitchen much later. Closing the door behind her, she dropped the car keys onto the counter and walked toward the stairs.

"Have a good visit?"

"Oh!" She spun around in the direction of Alec's voice. "You startled me." She clutched the neckline of her shirt.

"Sorry." He stepped out of the shadows. "I came down to get some water and heard you drive up. What are you doing back here?"

"I live here?"

He shrugged. "I just didn't think you'd come back tonight."

He didn't know how close he was to the truth.

Or maybe he did.

He was clad only in jeans, the ripple of hard muscle in his arms and chest apparent even in the semidarkness. She could sense the pure male aura that always seemed to surround him.

"Did Scotty settle in all right?"

"It took a while, but he's asleep."

Shea gave him a strained smile, nodded and together they climbed the stairs. When she stopped in front of the door to the bathroom, he proceeded down the hall without another word.

Stripping off her dirty clothes, she turned on the shower, stepped under the fine spray and let the hot water massage away the stress running rampant through her body. But she knew it would take more than hot water to make her relax. Alec had to go. Finding a way to make him leave was imperative and she had to do it quickly. She turned off the water and stepped out of the shower.

Her arm was tender from the bashing she'd taken from Bonnie Blue earlier. A large, reddish-purple bruise had begun to appear over much of her shoulder and upper arm. She carefully donned a worn-but-comfortable cotton T-shirt. After drying her hair, she applied moisturizer and brushed her teeth. With nothing more to keep her in the bathroom, she swallowed her trepidation and opened the door.

Two steps down the hall in the direction of the master bedroom, her feet suddenly reversed direction. Vivid in her mind's eye was the picture of lying in the bed, Alec's hands and mouth caressing her body, preparing her, priming her for the sex to follow. While she couldn't argue he oozed sex appeal, he was still a stranger: a cold man whose sole reason for being here was to take away her home.

Quickly, she made her way to her old bedroom, and quietly closed the door. With any luck, Alec would be asleep and never notice her absence. She pulled back the covers and climbed into bed.

She lay still, hopeful, watching the shadows from the leaves on the tree outside her window dance on the ceiling. She was so tired. Slowly, the tension began to leave, her muscles relaxed, and she closed her eyes and let sleep overtake her.

She was floating. Yet she could feel an iron brace holding her firmly against tremendous warmth. Groggily, she blinked open her eyes. She was being carried. Instantly she was awake, and just as quickly, she knew who was carrying her and where they were going.

Seconds later, Alec placed her on the large new bed. Before she could scramble away, he leaned over and placed his hands on either side of her, effectively preventing her escape.

"I told you in the beginning, you *will* sleep in my bed." She could hear the annoyance in his voice. "Unless you want to start packing right now, you'd better learn to deal with it."

Slowly he stood over her and Shea scurried to the far edge of the mattress, eyeing him with apprehension. He frowned, resting his hands on his hips.

"Where's your ring?"

The question threw her. "What ring?"

His mouth quirked. "Your *wedding* ring. Remember the little ceremony when you promised to love, honor and *obey*?"

"It's over there—" she nodded toward the dresser, deciding to ignore his taunt "—in that little box. I...didn't want to wear it while I worked in the barn."

He walked to the dresser and took the ring out of the case and then came back to the bed.

"Give me your hand."

With a grimace, she extended her left hand and he slipped the sparkling wedding band onto her third finger.

"Leave it on."

Without another word, he unzipped his jeans. Shea turned away, hugging the far side of the bed as close to the edge as she could get. He turned off the light and she felt the mattress shifting to accommodate his large frame. Then his heavy arm slid around her waist as he settled next to her.

"I missed you, Mrs. Morreston." His breath was warm against her ear, his voice deep and sexy. "I missed kissing you."

"Leave me alone."

"Remind me of what I missed."

"No." She tried to push his arm away, but her efforts were futile.

Alec's hand settled gently on her shoulder to turn her onto her back. She couldn't hold back a cry of pain when he touched the bruised area. He immediately released her. There was a faint movement and then light shattered the darkness.

"Let me see your shoulder. Take off your T-shirt."

She sat up. "It's nothing. Just a bruise."

"Now."

"No."

"Either you take it off or I will."

The hard lines of his face contained no sympathy, only determination. But she faced him with equal strength of purpose. "You have no right to make that demand. Nothing in the contract gives you the right. If I want to cut off my nose it's none of your concern."

"Does everything have to be a battle with you?"

She clamped her mouth shut and glared. He was about the most demanding man she'd ever met. Nothing in those rich golden eyes and handsome features showed the tiniest indication he would relent.

"I want to look at your shoulder," he stated evenly. "If you don't want me to see, then get dressed and I'll take you to the emergency room and have a doctor check it out. But I'm not going to ignore the fact that you're injured."

She searched his face, looking for any way to pierce the armor of his resolve. Finding none, she turned away from him and eased the injured arm out of the sleeve. Raising the tail of the shirt over her shoulder, she refused to meet his eyes.

Alec inspected her arm with a muttered curse. "You damn near broke your arm. You could have a fracture. I think you need to have it x-rayed. Why the hell didn't you say something?"

"I… It's not that bad." She shrugged. "It's not any more painful than being forced to live with you."

She heard him sigh. "What are you afraid of, Shea?" His raspy voice was compelling, tuning her senses to his every word. "I can feel you respond to me. I know my touch doesn't repulse you. Surely you've had sex before?"

Her head shot up, and she spun around on the bed to face him, pushing her arm back through the sleeve while glaring at him for his audacity. "I've *made love* before. To someone I knew and cared for very much." He watched her intently, his golden eyes again reminding her of a predator amusing himself with his prey while deciding if he was hungry. She turned away from his scrutiny. "I don't know you. And I certainly don't care for you."

He reached out, his fingers grasping her chin, turning her to him. His eyes held her there. "I have no intention of remaining celibate during our marriage. It'll be easier if you try to accept that. Accept me. The sooner you come to terms with it, the better off you'll be. Or you always have the option of leaving and bringing this craziness to an end."

Wrenching her chin from his grasp, she tried to swallow the feeling of doom welling in her throat. "I'm not going anywhere. Why don't you go visit one of your lady friends? I'm sure there must be *one* out there somewhere who isn't completely repulsed. Hell, you supposedly have money. Go buy one."

"Why would I do that when I already have a beautiful, desirable woman in my bed?"

He reached out to switch off the small table lamp, and she noted again his wide shoulders and large biceps. His bronzed skin gleamed in startling contrast to the white linens that barely covered his hips. She swallowed hard.

The light went out and the mattress shifted as he lay back.

"How long has it been, Shea?"

She jerked her head around to stare at him, even though now all she saw was a silhouette in the darkened room.

"How long has it been since a man held you in his arms, touched you…took you to the edge…made you crazy with wanting…then gave you release?"

His deep, throaty voice sent shivers down her spine.

"That's none of your business!" she snapped, her voice sounding hoarse to her own ears. His words planted images in her mind she didn't want to see.

"On the contrary, as your husband I think it's expressly my business."

"Think what you want." She was not about to discuss her sex life—or the lack of one—with him; she refused to give him any more ammunition. She lay down, facing away from him and adjusted her pillow.

"Why are you afraid of me?"

"I'm not."

He was still for so long, she found herself holding her breath in expectation of what he might do. But he made no further attempt to touch her or harass her. Shea lay very still, staring out into the darkness.

A man with Alec's experience would recognize the battle that raged within her every time he came close. She was painfully aware of her limited ability to withstand his sexual magnetism. She'd only ever been with one man and that experience was nothing close to what Alec's words described. His voice, his devastating good looks topped with his apparent expertise in bed made her traitorous body crave his touch. But common sense told her he would use her to his own end. Moreover, his tactics would be as low and cutthroat as he deemed necessary to prevail in this war of wills. She had to hold on.

The sounds of the night closed in around her. A distant rumble of thunder echoed the turbulence in her mind. Sleep, when it finally came, was uneasy. Visions swirled around in her head. The ranch, encased in a fog, began to disappear while the thunder rumbled overhead. Powerless to stop it, she cried out. Then she sensed comforting warmth surrounding her, holding her close and protected. The dream faded, and she knew peace.

Alec held the innocent warmth of her body against the ache of his own. The last time he'd held a woman—just held her—had been too long ago to remember. With other women, there was no reason to stay after their needs had been satisfied, and certainly no desire to hold them as they slept.

After Sondra's infidelities, he made certain his relationships stayed free of emotional entanglements. The women he chose knew the score. It was sex, mutually enjoyable, nothing more. With Shea, her claims to hate him one minute then passionately respond to his kiss the next affected him in ways he neither liked nor knew how to deal with. She was pretending. Acting. She had to be. She couldn't possibly be as naive as she was letting on.

A glimmer of speculation made him question if she could be for real. He hated that glimmer. He hated not knowing. But most of all, he hated the idea that he cared either way.

Sondra had acted completely innocent when she'd just come from the bed of another man. She'd shown him what she'd wanted him to see until the end when she'd displayed her true colors. He knew what women were capable of when they wanted something badly enough. Shea wanted this land. And, like Sondra, there were no rules as far as she was concerned. Nothing was out of bounds. Nothing off-limits. No holds barred until she got her way.

And he'd be every kind of fool if he didn't keep that at the forefront of his mind.

Seven

When Shea awoke in the predawn hours, the birds sang outside the window and for the first time in her life she scoffed at the sound.

Raising her head, she was shocked to realize she'd used Alec for a pillow. Immediately rolling away from him, she eased over to her side of the bed. Holding her breath in the hope her actions wouldn't wake him, she lifted the covers and swung her legs to the floor. His light snoring continued as she made her way to the door. Unable to resist she spared a quick glance at Alec. Even relaxed in sleep, he was an intimidating presence. She had to be strong. There was too much to lose if she didn't find a way to send him packing.

Entering her old room, she grabbed a clean shirt and a pair of jeans and made her way to the bathroom. Her right shoulder screamed as she pushed her arm through the sleeve of the fresh T-shirt. Her head felt as muddled as it had the night she'd tried to sleep in the barn. This was going to be a very long day.

She trudged to the kitchen, needing a strong cup of coffee. When she opened the pantry door to grab the coffee tin, she saw the jar of Yolanda's homemade hot sauce sitting on the same shelf. A smile kicked up the corners of her mouth as she grabbed both the coffee and the jar of liquid fire.

An hour later she sat sipping her coffee while the biscuits finished baking. Scotty had joined her and was busy eating his stack of pancakes. Her mind had finally cleared and was focused on any strategy that would get rid of her unwanted houseguest. She'd just stood to refill her cup when the subject of her thoughts walked into the room.

"Hi, Daddy!"

"G'morning, son. Shea. How'd you sleep?" Alec looked directly at his son.

"Good!"

Alec had anticipated Scotty waking him at least once due to the new and unfamiliar surroundings, but apparently he'd slept through the night. The tantalizing aroma of bacon and freshly brewed coffee stirred his appetite. He poured a cup and let his gaze settle on Shea, who was busy pulling a tray of golden-brown biscuits from the antique oven in the corner. Did she believe the old saying about the way to a man's heart being through his stomach? He smiled. If that's what she believed, who was he to correct her?

"Smells good. I never pictured you as Little Miss Homemaker." He smiled. "I think I could get used to this."

"Have a seat."

Pulling out the chair next to Scotty, Alec sat down. Within minutes, Shea set a plate of eggs and bacon on the table in front of him, followed by a basket of the biscuits.

"Aren't you going to eat?"

"Already have." She nodded to his plate. "You go ahead. Enjoy your breakfast."

With a brief nod of thanks, he dug in with relish. Shea stood to the side.

The first mouthful tasted as good as it looked. She was a damned fine cook. He shoveled a second helping of the spicy eggs into his mouth, but just as he swallowed, an odd sensation brought his chewing to a halt.

It wasn't the taste that gave him the first hint he'd been had. It was the pure liquid lava that scorched his mouth and throat and continued to burn all the way down to his toes that gave him his first clue.

His vision clouded with tears as he reached for his glass. An instant of surprised horror raced through his mind at the realization the glass was empty.

"Oops," Shea said in a bored tone. "I forgot to give you any juice. So sorry."

Grabbing one of the biscuits, still warm from the oven, he quickly bit down and almost broke a tooth in the process. One slam of the biscuit on the table told him he'd have done better biting into a rock.

And his mouth continued to burn.

"Are the biscuits hard?" She leaned over and lifted one out of the basket. "Huh. Guess I had the oven temperature too low."

He glowered at Shea, who still stood, a picture of innocence beside the table, before he ran for the sink.

Turning on the faucet, Alec leaned over and gulped at the cool tap. But instead of relieving the scalding sensation, the water actually increased the burning.

"Are you finished with your plate?" she asked from behind him, her tone indicating she saw nothing odd about her husband gulping water from the kitchen faucet while smoke had to be billowing out of his ears. "You didn't eat much of your eggs. I guess you weren't very hungry."

He could only glare at her, his tongue singed to numbness. She picked up the plate and dumped the remains into the sink. "I've got some errands to run. Jason needs some help with a couple of chores. I told him you'd meet him behind the main barn right after breakfast."

"Chores?" he asked, looking at her suspiciously, before reaching for a napkin to wipe his watery eyes and running nose. "Like what?"

"Some fences need mending. Stalls have to be cleaned. A couple of old trees, downed during the last storm, are blocking the north gate. They'll need to be chopped, split for firewood, hauled to the house and stacked."

"Anything else?"

She smiled. "Jason has a list."

The sound of steady clicking challenged the silence in the old house as Shea stepped into the kitchen. She'd intended to start supper as soon as she got home, but curiosity made her set the sack of green beans and new potatoes—a gift from Leona—on the table. A frown crossed her face as she followed the sound out of the kitchen and down the hall. Pushing open the door to her office, she was dumbstruck at the sight of Alec sitting behind the old desk typing on a laptop, his files and papers strewn all over, her ledgers and ranch records pushed to one side. Immediately her temper flared.

"What do you think you're doing?"

He spared her a quick glance. "Working."

"You're in *my* office."

"There wasn't another one."

"You can't just barge in here and—"

"I have my own work to do. I'm not here solely to be your hired hand." He glanced at his palm and she couldn't miss seeing the multitude of blisters. He grimaced and then pulled open the drawer with his fingers. "I need a ruler."

She crossed her arms in a defensive gesture and refused to respond.

Alec shut the drawer. "Look. My own work can't come to a crashing halt simply because I've changed my address."

"Well, neither can mine! I can't work around you. You've buried my ledger underneath your junk!"

With a barely concealed sigh of frustration, he nodded his head. "All right, *dear*," he said sarcastically. "If you're going to work in your ledger, may I *please* set you up at the kitchen table long enough for me to send some emails?"

Emails? She relaxed her stance. His sarcasm was about

to change into something much more enthralling and she had a front row seat.

"Emails?" She saw him nod as he stood and began to gather her books. "How are you going to send emails?"

"What do you mean, how am I going to send…?" he began, his words dying in his mouth as realization settled in. "Tell me you have an internet connection."

Smiling, she shook her head. "Sorry."

"Well, this is just great." He sat back, rubbed his neck and then flinched from the blisters on his palms. "My cell is useless out here. I can't get through to my office on your landline until some talker named Ms. Hoover finishes the call to her sister."

"That would be Gladys."

"And now no internet."

He tossed the pencil onto the desk and stood up. "This is the twenty-first century and you people are still using stone knives and bear skins. It's amazing old Gladys doesn't break out the drums."

"Hey, if you don't like it…"

Muttering under his breath, Alec stomped past her and limped out of the room, the soreness in his body apparent. Score two points for her side.

The next few days were a repeat of the same routine. After Alec carefully tested the food before eating his breakfast, he and Jason would leave to complete the multitude of tasks needing to be done around the ranch. Because Shea had so much to do to prepare for the roundup—decisions only she could make—Hank had slowly transitioned to the role of part-time babysitter, a job both he and little Scotty seemed to enjoy.

Alec had taken time out to arrange for a wireless internet service. She'd seen the work trucks go up and down the main road indicating the installation of a new communications tower. She didn't even want to guess how he'd pulled that off. Or how much it had cost. He'd commandeered one of the unused bedrooms upstairs for his office. A new desk and chair had been delivered. After a long day of physical labor with Jason, he would often spend hours in his new office, sometimes working well into the night. Phone calls came in at all hours to his cell phone. If Alec wasn't there, the call would transfer to an answering service somewhere. Shea often went to sleep listening to him speak in various languages and wondered if he worked with people all over the world. She had to admit, having him at the Bar H was not turning out to be the total nightmare she'd feared. At least not yet.

A couple of weeks after Alec began working with Jason, Shea spotted the younger ranch hand as he walked toward his truck to go home at the end of the day. She'd been curious if Alec had been making an honest effort to lend a hand. She ran to catch up with Jason before he pulled out of the driveway.

"He's awesome," Jason replied to her question, grinning. "Alec works as hard as I do. No breaks. No hesitation to take on any job that needs doing. He's a great guy. You should have married him a long time ago."

"Thanks." She tried to keep the sarcasm out of her tone. "See you tomorrow."

As Jason backed his truck out of the gravel parking area, Shea wondered what Alec was up to. Why would he work so hard to make repairs on a ranch he wanted to level?

She rounded the corner and walked in through the back door of the old farmhouse. She found the subject of her thoughts standing in the kitchen, a bunch of wildflowers clutched in his fist. Her eyebrows shot up at the sight of the big, powerful man clutching a handful of wilting flowers.

"I picked these just before we headed back to the barn." He held the bouquet out to her. "I thought…well, maybe they might look nice on the table." She heard a touch of awkwardness in his voice, which was completely out of character for Alec. That surprised her as much as the offering of flowers. "The west pasture was full of them," he added. "Like a multicolored blanket almost as far as the eye could see. It was amazing. Anyway…"

Stunned, she accepted the offering. She looked from the blooms to Alec and couldn't stop the smile that widened her lips. It was a thoughtful gesture and one she never would have expected from him.

"Thank you," she said earnestly. "And you're right—the flowers are remarkable this time of year. You might want to stay clear of the blue ones. They're the state flower and I don't think we're supposed to pick them."

"Ah," Alec nodded his head, indicating message received. "Okay. Well, I need a shower."

As he left the room, Shea looked at the colorful bouquet. The mixed colors of yellow, orange, pink and blue would indeed make a pretty table setting. She selected a crystal glass from the cabinet, added water and arranged the blooms before placing the small arrangement in the center of the table.

Alec Morreston had brought her flowers.

He probably had a hidden agenda in there somewhere, but that thought couldn't diminish the delight she felt receiving the small gift. She'd be wise to keep up her guard and watch him like a starving hawk would a mouse. He had to be up to something. But for now, she would enjoy the flowers and consider this nothing more than a thoughtful gesture.

Later, when they all sat down for dinner, Alec spoke with enthusiasm about what they'd accomplished that day, asking her questions about the ranch setup or the livestock, but stopping just short of making any suggestions. Why try to improve something that, if he had his way, wouldn't be here in a year? But it let her see more of the man he was beneath the business suit. Locked away inside her where no one could see, a seed of respect for him had begun to take root and grow.

As she gathered the empty plates from the table and placed them in the soapy water, Shea was suddenly overcome with an intense wave of sadness. Between the gestures of kindness, the unspoken treaty between them for Scotty's sake and the camaraderie that had developed among Alec, Hank and the other ranch hands, it gave the illusion of one big happy family. The evening meals were a time of friendly banter, sharing humorous stories of the past and ideas for a future that possibly would never be. Even little Scotty played into the role of her loving son. And she was beginning to love him. She couldn't keep herself from forming a bond with such an adorable, bright child.

Each day seemed to intensify the illusion and it was becoming more difficult to remember that this was not a family. It was not a time for joking. There should be no camaraderie. This was not a game of pretend. It was war. And it was very real. A mandatory sentence forcing two opposing, equally determined individuals into a life-changing competition requiring constant stamina and strength of mind to win the grand prize, all within preposterous directives set up two hundred years ago by individuals unknown and for reasons she couldn't fathom. It was clearly a chapter out of a Stephen King novel.

At times she felt herself slipping into the illusion, letting it envelop her, as though something deep inside wanted it to become real with a desperation that was off the scale. The dangers of this were obvious. She had to remain focused. She had to remember that this illusion of a happy home with a handsome, caring husband and loving child was not reality. And never would be.

* * *

The ledger remained open awaiting a final calculation, but it was just a closing formality. She already knew the profit margin, while small, was clearly there. As long as the beef prices didn't take a sudden plunge before they shipped, the ranch would have a profitable year.

A soft knocking from the open doorway pulled her attention from the columns of figures. She glanced up to see Alec stroll into the room. His gaze rested first on her, then shifted to the collage of framed photographs hanging neatly on the wall to his left.

"Mind if I just look around?"

She shrugged. "Go ahead."

She tried to return her attention to the ledger but his presence presented a distraction she couldn't easily ignore.

"I noticed these right after I arrived." He scanned the wall of framed photographs. "Some of these pictures are really old."

"I think the oldest ones are from the mid-1800s."

Pictures of cowboys with their horses, branding operations, women dressed in styles portraying Western fashion almost two hundred years ago.

"Is this your father?" He pointed to a picture in the upper right corner of the grouping.

"Yes."

"Who are the two men with the longhorn?"

"My grandfather and his brother," she answered, never taking her eyes from the computer screen. She didn't need to. She knew the snapshots by heart. "They were one of seven families credited with bringing the longhorn back from near extinction."

Alec moved farther down the wall. "There's a kid on a horse getting some kind of award," he said, observing another picture. "Is it you?"

"Yeah." She saw no reason to elaborate.

"And what about this one?"

Shea glanced at the wall. He pointed to picture of a child astride a large dapple-gray thoroughbred. "That's me on Sir Raleigh at the hunter-jumper competition at Fair Park in Dallas. I was about twelve." She nodded to the next picture. "You might recognize the person in that one."

Alec leaned toward the picture. "Leona?"

She nodded, unable to restrain a smile. "It was taken several years ago during a Fourth of July party."

"She looks…different."

"She was smashed. Somebody spiked her watermelon punch."

Alec grinned. "These are fascinating pictures. I feel as though I'm looking at a wall in a cowboy history museum."

He glanced at Shea. In surprising contrast to the usual glare she sent in his direction, she was smiling. He walked over to the old leather wing-backed chair that faced the massive oak desk and sat down.

"When I was a teenager, there was a fairly large stable a few miles from our summer house in Saratoga County in upstate New York," he said, leaning back and resting one booted ankle on the other knee. "The Tall Pine Stables." He shook his head. "I haven't thought about it in years. My dad was determined his sons would learn the value of a dollar. I was given the choice of working in his office during the summer—" Alec nodded at the ledger "—which meant sitting behind a desk. Or I could find my own job. Most of my friends got summer work flipping burgers, sacking groceries or caddying at the country club. I was lucky enough to find work mucking out horse stalls."

"You?" Her eyebrows shot up and her eyes grew wide.

Alec chuckled. "Yeah, me. Not fun, as I'm sure you know. But I loved the horses, so I stuck it out. Went back the next two summers and the second year the owner began to supplement my pay with the bonus of exercising a few

of the thoroughbreds. It was…amazing. I loved their spirit.
I swore I would have one of my own someday."

"And did you?"

"Nah." He shrugged. "Just never worked out."

He envied Shea her life and the way she'd been raised.
Close to the land and nature. It had always beckoned him,
but he'd never stopped long enough to heed the call.

"That's really too bad." Her voice was soft, as though
she was truly sorry he'd never seen that dream realized.
"You've still got time. And I think Scott would love it. He
seems to have inherited your love of horses."

Alec nodded. "Yeah. So it would appear." He was
thoughtful for a moment. "I might never have known if
we hadn't come here. Maybe I can work something out."
He stood from the chair. "I'll get out of here and let you
finish your work. Guess I'd better go and check on Scott."
He walked to the door.

"Alec?"

"Yeah." He faced her.

"Thanks for sharing that with me."

She smiled and while it was cautious and hesitant, nonetheless something deep inside him felt very good.

It was almost midnight when Shea stretched and stood
up, flexing her tired muscles. After Alec's visit, it had taken
quite a while to regain her concentration on the work she'd
needed to finish. To say she'd been surprised by his story
of working summers at a stable was an understatement.
She never would have pictured Alec Morreston mucking
stalls. Or riding thoroughbreds. His professed love of horses
seemed to contradict his intent to close the ranch. It was yet
another layer of the complex man. It would be prudent to
watch him even closer. Apparently there was much more
to Alec than she'd originally thought and he could use any
accrued knowledge against her, which brought back the

earlier sadness and added to the growing stress she already was feeling.

At times, she felt as if she was a stranger in her own home. She wasn't used to not trusting people, to always being on guard, having to watch her every action and word, being alert to anything Alec did or saw as potentially giving him leverage to take the ranch. It was like walking a tightrope and even though she would never admit it aloud, it was taking its toll. Her nerves were shot to hell and frustration was building. She had to wonder how much longer this situation would last before it blew sky high.

With a sigh, she turned off the computer, returned the ledger to the bottom drawer of the desk, flipped off the light and left the office. A hot shower sounded wonderful. The few minutes of relaxation it would provide were definitely needed.

In the bathroom, she turned on the water and peeled off her clothes. Soon steam began to cloud the room as hot water jettisoned out of the nozzle.

Stepping into the shower, she reached for the bottle of shampoo. Empty. Muttering to herself, she stepped back out of the shower to grab a new bottle from the cabinet.

She'd not taken more than three steps when a slick spot on the tile floor sent both feet shooting out from under her. She landed in a sprawling, floundering heap, hitting the floor so hard she swore the earth shook from the force of it.

For a few moments, she lay in stunned silence, then slowly clambered to her feet and gingerly made her way to the cabinet. Grabbing the new bottle of shampoo, she limped back to the shower.

As she applied the soap, working up a good lather, she noticed the water didn't seem quite as hot as it had been just seconds before. With her eyes tightly closed, she fumbled with the taps, trying to adjust the temperature. It wasn't until she had turned off the cold completely that she realized there was no more hot water. At that very moment, the old pipes began to rumble and groan as if building in momentum, and half a heartbeat later, a spray of water from the icy depths of the well hit her squarely in the face.

A squeal of surprise tore from her throat. Sputtering and coughing, she managed to withstand the frigid temperature long enough to rinse out the shampoo, then immediately turned off the tap. Teeth chattering, goose bumps covering her skin, she stepped from the shower, careful to avoid the slick spot this time, and edged her way around the room to the linen cabinet.

She stared in disbelief. The shelves were empty. This morning, there had been at least a dozen bath towels in the linen closet. Now, all that remained were several washcloths and one hand towel.

Dripping wet and shivering, she grabbed the hand towel and began blotting the water from her skin and hair. This was no accident. It had the Morreston name written all over it. Oh, how she hated that damned contract. She wished she could go back in time and do something vile to the ancestor who'd added that insane clause. She combed the tangles from her hair, stepped into her panties, pulled on an oversize T-shirt and slowly counted to ten.

It wasn't long enough.

The bedroom was in darkness but in the soft glow from the yard light outside, Shea could see Alec's silhouette sprawled diagonally across the bed. Still shivering, she walked to the far side. His large frame lay on top of the covers and try as she might, she couldn't dislodge enough of the top sheet and blanket from under his sleeping form to give her even a small amount of warmth.

Suddenly, the urge to whack the horrible man with a blunt object overcame her common sense. A thirst for revenge compelled her to grab the edge of a pillow, yank it from under his head, raise it high and slam it down on top of the sleeping man with all the force she could muster.

"Hey!"

Again the pillow came down on his head.

"What the hell…?"

And again.

"Goddammit, Shea!" He caught her wrist and pulled her down onto the bed, fighting to control her flailing legs and arms. "Stop it! What the hell's the matter with you?"

"*You*. You're what's the matter with me!" she snarled. "Let me go!"

She pushed against him and tried to twist free. He easily controlled her efforts, throwing one leg over hers, catching and holding both her hands above her head and firmly pressing the parts in between against his muscled length.

"I want to know what brought this on."

"Nothing. Just…nothing. Let me go."

"Not happening."

She struggled against him, making one last all-out effort to free her hands before giving up and glaring at him through the darkness. She saw his focus move from her eyes to her mouth seconds before he lowered his head and covered her lips with his own. She tried to turn away, but he effortlessly held her in place. His lips were full and warm and totally enticing. Her mind let go of her earlier frustration and focused on Alec. His slow, lazy kiss made the need to get away from him seem not quite as important as it had seconds ago.

He raised his head and their gazes met through the dim glow from the lights at the barn. It was as though he was offering her a choice. When she didn't move away, he returned to her lips without saying a word, his mouth claiming hers in a deep and passionate kiss. His tongue entered her, filled her, and gone was any want for him to stop. With a sigh, she gave up the struggle. The passion escalated to raw, hungry need.

Her oversize T-shirt was twisted and stretched tightly over her breasts. She felt the warmth of his hand move up her side to gently squeeze the soft flesh. He lowered his head, placing his mouth over one taut nipple, licking and sucking through the thin material. Shea drew air deep into her lungs, her breasts swelling under his touch. His hot mouth moved to the other breast, bringing it to the same throbbing ache, an ache that shot straight to her core.

Taking one of her hands, Alec directed it down between their bodies, placing her fingers against his sex, holding it there when she would have drawn away. "No. Feel me, Shea. Feel what you do to me." His voice was low, gritty, as though the tight rein on his emotions was about to shatter.

She became lost in the sensation. Her hand couldn't fully encompass his girth, but he throbbed under her touch. His lips returned to hers, hungry, wanting. His hand slid down her belly, not pausing until he was cupping her most sensitive flesh. "Open your legs for me, Shea," he instructed, his voice raw. "Do it."

The final remnants of hesitation dissolved as she obeyed, raising one leg, allowing him access to the most private part of her. His skilled hands increased her need for penetration to a level of near desperation. All other motion ceased, her body paralyzed, completely enraptured by what he was doing.

Alec was on fire and close to losing it before he ever got inside of her. He wanted her with desperation he'd never before experienced. The sweet smell of her arousal flooded his senses. Her breath rushed in and out as her hands encircled his neck, holding him to her while her hips pushed against his throbbing erection, leaving no doubt in his mind she needed more.

Seconds, maybe less, before he permanently changed the entire situation, the cell phone he'd put on the nightstand began to ring. Its loud, shrill robotic tone infused the moment with cold reality.

All motion stopped. Breathing hard, he opened his eyes. *What in the hell was he doing?*

With a shuddering regret, Alec rolled to his side, his body protesting painfully, refusing to downshift. He had almost done it again. Making love to Shea was not going to accomplish anything except temporarily easing the pain of arousal. It would open a box full of complications neither one of them needed. He had little doubt that Shea didn't normally partake in one-night flings. This was something they would both regret, albeit for very different reasons, in the light of day.

The ringing stopped. As he lay next to her, willing his breathing to slow, she turned away from him, rolling onto her side. She didn't speak, and damn if he knew what to say. He'd honestly never been in this situation, wanting a woman beyond comprehension but knowing it was absolutely wrong, even as she lay in the bed next to him. He swallowed hard. He had to offer her something. He couldn't ignore her emotions.

"Shea?"

She was quiet for so long, he thought she wasn't going to answer. Then her voice reached him through the darkness.

"I understand, Alec."

Then maybe she could explain it to him.

"It's this whole horrible situation." Her voice sounded strained, as though she was struggling not to cry. He sensed a motion. Was she wiping the tears from her eyes? "I no longer know what's right and what isn't. I lost the map. I don't know how I should feel or what I should do. I want my life back. I want my dad not to have died." She drew a shaky breath. "I want to feel, even for a minute, that I'm not a stranger in my own house. That I'm not alone and fighting against the entire world."

"Hey." Alec gently pulled her into his arms, determined to relieve some of the heartache he had no doubt caused. Her head rested on his shoulder. She offered no resistance. "You're not taking on the world," he responded. "Just me. And from this side of the bed, you're doing a pretty damn good job."

He sensed rather than saw her smile and she sniffed back the tears. Beyond her beauty, she was an honest, caring woman who hadn't asked for any of this. He felt the urge to tell her she could have the ranch. But he couldn't. There was already too much invested, both time and money. There were too many people counting on this project for jobs and investors expecting something for their venture. For the first time since coming here, Alec wished he could just walk away. Let Shea's life return to normal. Hell, let both of them return to doing what made them happy.

That thought brought him up short. When *had* he last been happy? Before coming here, when was the last time he'd slept throughout the night without waking to pace the floor at 3:00 a.m.? How long had he been working such long hours that he didn't know if it was day or night? When had he taken the time to reflect on his childhood and his fishing excursions with Grandpa Jacob? When had he spent as much quality time with Scotty? Everything here seemed to move at a much slower pace. But he felt at home here, like a figurine that had found its way back into the mold. And it all revolved around Shea and this ranch. All the good and positive feelings.

"Shea?" Alec lowered his face to the top of her head. She had fallen asleep in his arms, her head on his shoulder, her arm resting across his stomach. He loved the softness of her hair, how it always smelled like the sweet blooms of the Ligustrum trees that grew in abundance here. He lay back on the pillow, his fingers playing idly in the silky strands of her hair, closed his eyes and drew her intoxicating aroma deep into his lungs. The softness of her breasts pressed against him, her breathing gentle on his skin. It felt so right. While this moment in time was nothing life changing, he knew it was a time he wouldn't soon forget.

For almost a month, he'd lain in this bed night after night, taunted by the temptation of her sleeping next to him. What had happened to his brilliant notion that he would have her gone in a few days? Things had changed. *He* had changed. He wanted her to like him. She stirred him as no woman ever had and they hadn't even been intimate. Although they'd damn sure come close. Too close.

What he wanted from Shea was more than sex—and that was a first for him. And he knew because of the land situation and that damned contract he had little-to-no hope of anything more between them ever coming to pass.

Eight

Shea had just finished drying the breakfast dishes when Scotty ran into the kitchen, eyes wide, excitement pouring out of every pore of his small frame.

"Shea!" He stood next to the table, looking as though he was going to explode. The fingers of his small hands knotted together and then unknotted over and over.

"What is it, sweetie?"

"Hank had to go into town and Daddy doesn't have to work with Jason on account of Jason taking his wife to a doctor and Daddy said he didn't have to work at his other job and we can go fishing and I've never been fishing but he doesn't know where the fishes are." He took a breath. "So...Daddy said to come and ask where you keep 'em."

She couldn't stop the grin from covering her face. Only one place came immediately to mind. Grady's Gulch. About a mile to the north, just past the lake, a ravine wound its way toward the Red River. In one spot near a huge granite bolder, the banks drastically curved, creating a deep cavity that contained some of the best fishing anybody could ever hope to find. Shea knew a moment of hesitation. Few people knew of the spot. Did she really want to share this special spot with Alec? But a second glimpse into Scotty's hopeful eyes made the decision.

"I know just the place," she said, smiling, as his eyes grew even larger. She bent over and grabbed a large empty coffee can from the cabinet under the sink. "Take this to your dad and tell him to dig for some worms in that shady area near the well house. I'll get the fishing poles and meet you guys at the truck."

Scott bolted out of the kitchen and tore down the path to the barn yelling "Daddy!" the whole way.

Within an hour, the three of them were bouncing their way across the meadow. As Shea pulled into a tranquil spot under one of the giant oak trees and killed the engine, Alec immediately heard the sound of rushing water. A small trail led in that direction. Grabbing the poles and can of worms, he nodded for Shea to lead the way.

While she spread the old blanket in a shady spot next to the river, Alec baited the hook. With a cork firmly attached to the line, he swung it out over the water and handed the pole to Scotty.

"Just watch the cork, son. If you see it dip under the water, raise the pole really fast with a quick yank." Scotty nodded his understanding, his eyes not straying from the bobbing red-and-white ball floating toward the opposite bank.

When Alec turned to the blanket, Shea was staring up at him as though he'd grown an extra set of ears. "What?" he asked and looked down at his shirt.

"Nothing."

"Not fair."

She shrugged. "I just find it amazing you know how to bait a hook and can give instructions on how to fish with a cork."

Joining her on the well-used coverlet, he leaned back against the large tree trunk. "You think because I live in a city I've never been fishing?"

"Something like that. At least not without some fancy rigging."

"Well let me set the record straight. When I was just

about Scotty's age, my grandparents lived in a rural area a lot like this. I spent my summers with them. Gramps was big on fishing. He would cut his own cane pole, tie a string to the end, dig some worms and off we would go." Alec couldn't help but chuckle at the thought.

"You talk like those memories are…like they're special to you."

"They are." Alec frowned, not immediately understanding why she would say that.

"Yet you've never taken Scott fishing?"

Alec dropped his head and nodded. "You're right. Kept telling myself I would take him someplace special next week or next month but something always came up and it just never happened." And it was a regret Alec had carried with him for a long time.

"Well, you're doing it now."

He nodded and gave her a smile. "Yeah, I am. Thanks to you."

Shea shrugged as though none of this was her doing. Alec knew different. "How did you know about this place?"

"Because right over there—" she pointed to a granite boulder on the other side of the river "—is where I caught my first fish. Not many know about this place. Dad and his father and uncle guarded it as though the bottom was paved in gold. People tried for years to find out where Dad always managed to catch all the fish he would bring to a fish fry. I don't think they ever did."

Alec tilted his head. "But you were willing to share it with us."

Shea held his gaze, neither speaking nor nodding, and for a few brief seconds in time, the rest of the world ceased to exist. She had placed her trust in him, shared one of the special places in her life and some happy memories she treasured. She'd given Scotty a day of fun and Alec a small measure of relief from the guilt of not spending enough time with his son. He felt a kinship with the rich earth, with the cool water as it splashed against the huge boulders on its way downstream, the towering trees providing shade, their tallest branches catching and swaying in the gentle breeze. In spite of the animosity between them and her fierce determination to keep this ranch, Shea had shared something special with a virtual stranger who would take it all away.

Alec swallowed hard and closed his eyes. He wasn't used to her world and accepting acts of kindness wasn't in the game plan. Her small benevolences knocked him completely off balance. Other than Scotty, his mother and brother, he wasn't used to trusting people. But in that moment, he knew he could trust Shea with anything, including his son. And a shadow of guilt for what he was attempting to do with regard to the ranch seemed to put a dark cloud over the day.

"Daddy! It's gone! The fishies got it!"

Quickly getting to his feet, Alec hurried over to assist his son with the pole. In a matter of seconds, Scotty had landed his first fish. When he held it up, the fish still thrashed about on the end of the line and the boy wasn't certain exactly what to do with it. They should have brought a camera…

"Alec, do you have your cell phone?"

"Yeah, why?"

"Does it take pictures?"

Alec grinned. Of course. Why hadn't he thought of it? "It most certainly does."

Reaching into his pocket, he pulled out the small black phone, changed the settings and handed it to Shea.

She snapped away as father and son posed for a "first fish" picture, then continued to take shots as Alec patiently removed the hook and held the prize catch for Scott to touch.

"How about we let it go today?" Alec suggested. "Then

you can come back and catch it again sometime when we want to have fish for supper."

Without a word, Scotty vigorously nodded his head, clearly still amazed at the entire process.

They lingered next to the small river until the sun dropped low in the sky. It was as though they'd formed a truce and had silently declared this a place of neutrality where legal contracts and land development had no admittance. While Scotty waited for his next fish to grab the hook, Shea and Alec exchanged stories of their youth. The more she told him about special places and times on the ranch, the tighter the knot in his belly grew.

His planned development wouldn't reach this far out from the Red River. Maybe there was something he could do to let her keep at least part of her home. For months, the investors had been maneuvering about where they wanted this or that and adding more and more to the overall size of the project. It was his project and he maintained control, but his professional integrity insisted he consult with them on any major changes. For the first time he seriously considered reducing the overall scope of the project. It was certainly worth looking into.

The telephone rang as Shea entered the kitchen the next morning. She grabbed it on the second ring.

"Morning!" Leona's familiar voice hailed her from the other end of the line.

"I guess," she replied.

"Everything all right?"

"I suppose. So far. I haven't seen Alec or Scotty this morning."

"Well, I called to tell you they're both over here. Rode over with Hank. Alec is getting a tour of the spread, and the boy is with my grandson, Cody. They're playing with the new puppies."

"Oh, that's right. Maggie had her pups, didn't she?"

"Yep," Leona confirmed. "Did you remember tonight is the party to celebrate Ms. Annie's birthday?"

Annie Philpot was considered the matriarch of the Calico Springs ranching community. She'd married and lost two fine husbands, and then, by herself, had raised her nine children and carried on the tradition of producing fine horses and prime beef cattle. Through it all, she'd still found time to care for the friends and neighbors she loved. In times of sickness or when a new baby was about to make its presence known, Miss Annie had been there. In recent years, she'd reached out more via telephone than personal visits, but nonetheless her heart remained with her extended family.

"Oh, Leona, I'd completely forgotten."

"Figured you might have, what with the way your life has been here lately. It's been a while since you've seen everyone. Most of 'em are about to bust open with curiosity about Alec. Try and make it over here, if you can."

"Absolutely." She would have plenty of time to make a pie. Everyone always brought a dish or dessert to these gatherings. But something else tugged at her mind.

"Leona, does anyone know?" If rumors were flying about Alec taking her ranch and his plans for the land, she needed to know before they walked into the party.

A numbing pause followed the question.

"You mean about Alec?"

"Yeah."

"No. At least nothing's been said to me. Whatever he's planning, he's kept to himself. There has been some talk of a big entertainment complex gonna be built across the river in Oklahoma. People are generally either excited about the idea or don't much believe it. Is that what he's doing?"

"I honestly don't know." Alec had never told her and she hadn't asked. Shea wasn't sure she wanted to know. Whatever he had in mind was not going to happen and that was as far as her mind had gone on the subject. Let him build his magical kingdom in the adjacent state if he wanted. Just keep it off her ranch land and out of the community. "Thanks, Leona. We'll see you about eight."

By six o'clock Alec had returned and by seven thirty they were on their way to Leona's house. At least fifty adults and maybe a dozen kids were already enjoying the festivities when they arrived. The aroma of hickory smoke from a huge grill invited all new arrivals to bring their appetites around to the back of the house. Several long tables were set up, complete with red-checkered tablecloths. Shea placed her pie on the table with the other desserts.

One hello led to another and another until most of the party guests had met Shea's new husband. Alec dutifully shook hands and repeatedly answered the questions of the evening: "Where are you from?" and "How did you meet?" He surprised her by responding to their inquiries in a manner both believable and flattering to her.

In essence, he lied.

They paid their respects to the guest of honor, wishing Miss Annie a most happy eighty-ninth birthday. Then they joined Hank and Leona in the chow line and came away with their plates heavily laden with home-cooked fare. Scotty wanted to eat with Leona's grandson and several other kids his age. A table had been set up just for them.

When darkness fell, candles and lanterns cast their soft glow over the crowd. Several strands of white twinkle lights strung in the lower tree branches gave a strange, almost mystical, ambience to the festivities. With an area under the lights cleared for dancing, couples filled the space as the soft melody of a country ballad drifted through the cooling night air.

At the edge of the sphere of soft light, some of the children, including Scott, held sparklers, running back and forth, waving their arms, making circles and glowing formations against the darkness. Their laughter blended with the music and the cheerful mood of the adults, most of them lifelong friends, who'd gathered to celebrate another year of life of one of their own.

Shea knew total relaxation for the first time in a very long time. She sat quietly, eyes closed, listening to the music. Unexpectedly, a warm hand touched her shoulder. She looked up to find Alec standing beside her.

"Dance with me."

Without waiting for an answer, he took her hand and led her to the edge of the dancing couples, drawing her into his arms.

The music flowed in a soft, slow tempo. His arms encircled her, holding her close while they moved together to the rhythm of the song. It seemed the most natural thing in the world to rest her head against his shoulder. She closed her eyes, intoxicated by the musky scent of his cologne, warmed by the sheer strength of the arms around her.

This is so wrong. She shouldn't be dancing with this man—shouldn't be taking pleasure in his arms. By getting to know Alec, by seeing him as something other than the enemy, it was becoming more and more difficult to ignore her growing attraction to him. She liked him. A lot, in fact. Amazingly, the realization wasn't so painful.

As they danced, his thigh intermittently rubbed against her lower belly. She found herself holding her breath when he moved away until another shift in their movements again caused the hard contours of his body to press against her.

His fingers threaded through her hair, cupping the back of her head as he gently encouraged her gaze to meet his. She saw the flames of controlled passion in his darkening eyes before he lowered his head and settled his mouth on hers.

The kiss was pure seduction. A ball of searing heat shot

straight to the juncture between her legs while the world around them ceased to exist.

Alec made a slight adjustment and his swollen shaft pressed solidly against her belly. For a moment, instinct took over and she succumbed to the blinding need to forget everything but the urge to satisfy the ache his touch created. She gave in to her body's natural reaction and pushed against him. She heard his sharp intake of breath followed by a low growl. He lowered his hands to her hips, pulling her solidly against him, and wanton desire scorched the skin beneath her jeans.

The loud snapping of firecrackers close by made her jump. She tore her lips from his as reality came crashing back with ferocity. It was as if someone had suddenly turned up the volume to the music and the voices around them. Her eyes lingered on his mouth. The temptation to return and seek the pleasures it offered was overwhelming.

Blinking, she stepped back and looked around her, feeling as if she'd just come back from another time and place. Desperately she willed her mind to reengage.

They were in the midst of some twenty dancing couples. Glancing around, she was thankful to see that no one appeared aware of the sensual drama unfolding in their midst. She chanced another look at Alec's face, and in the depths of his eyes she saw awareness of her internal battle. He knew how close she was to losing.

"I should go…and help Leona."

"Leona has all the help she needs." He gently smoothed a stray lock of hair back from her face. "Let's go home."

His deep, husky invitation was almost her undoing. "I…" Her eyes roamed over his face while he waited patiently for her decision. He wanted her. He wasn't using coercion or bribery. There were no threats. He was putting it out on the table and she could say yes or she could say no.

She couldn't make love to Alec. Could she? He was still

her enemy. Wasn't he? She didn't believe in casual sex. For Shea, intimacy had to be between two people who honestly cared for each other. And even if she felt that way toward Alec, could she justify one night of ecstasy with a man who was bent on destroying everything she had?

"I...I've got to go." She pushed out of his arms, walked in the direction of Leona's house and didn't look back.

Shea wasn't sure what was happening between them, but at the very least, she knew she already had broken her number one directive: hating Alec Morreston.

"It looks like you two are having a good time," Leona remarked as she entered the kitchen. She handed Shea a dishtowel.

Shea nodded and picked up a plate, unable to meet Leona's eyes. "I guess."

"Things going any better?"

She shrugged. Alec wasn't the adversary she'd initially expected. Either his tactics weren't as cutthroat as she'd first feared, or the man was tremendously subtle and highly skilled at manipulation. Probably both. But since his return from New York with his son, she'd glimpsed another side of the man. Even Scotty was a revelation, providing insight into the complexities of Alec's character. It was as if he were two different people. One was the enemy, a cold and ruthless man bent on destroying everything. The other was a caring and loving father who had gained her respect and was well on his way to becoming someone she cared about.

In spite of what he'd threatened that day in Ben's office, in spite of his determination to force her from the land, he'd given her time. Conversely, the more time he gave her, the more she contemplated what it would be like to love such a man. Lovers with no future, engaged in an affair that was sure to end badly. Who did that? Was she so foolish to fall in love with the very man who would take away everything she'd ever loved?

She picked up another plate and began to rub it with the towel. Leona snatched it from her hand.

"You're drying a dirty plate," she said, her eyes narrowing. "You haven't heard a word I've said for the last five minutes. Do I get to guess where your mind is?"

Blushing, Shea shook her head.

"Just be careful," Leona cautioned.

Shea nodded and reached for a clean plate.

With the few nondisposable dishes washed and dried, and the remaining food covered and put away, Shea stepped outside. She spotted Hank and Alec and walked in that direction. Detecting her presence next to him, Alec reached out to her, his arm settling around her shoulders. "Scott and Cody are going to sleep in their fort tonight. Steve Laughton said he'd stay out here with them and make sure they got inside the house if it starts to rain. Are you ready to go?"

"I guess. Good night, Hank."

The old cowboy nodded and touched his finger to his hat. Alec's hand remained at the back of her neck as they walked to his car. He seated her inside the luxury sedan, then took his place behind the wheel. She sat back in the plush leather seat, her head on the cushioned rest while the car easily ate up the miles to the Bar H. She glanced at the multitude of lights on the front console, then let her eyes move to the large man behind the wheel. He caught her glance and returned it.

"You have some nice neighbors," he said. "I enjoyed meeting them."

"They liked you, too." She turned her head to stare out into the seemingly endless shadows of the night. "It's too bad…"

"It's too bad…what?" he prompted.

"Well, I can't help but wonder what their reaction will be when they discover your plans for my ranch and ultimately this area. Most of these folks are third- and fourth-

generation farmers and ranchers. They won't take kindly
to some out-of-towner plopping a housing development in
the center of their grazing land or paving their neighbor's
pasture for a parking lot."

Shea chanced a quick glance in his direction. Alec continued to look straight ahead, seemingly without emotion,
but in the dim light from the driver's panel, she noted a
brief grimace cross his features.

"For your information, I have no intention of building
a housing development here or anywhere else. That's not
what I do."

"Maybe not, but you're a commercial developer," she
stated, daring him to deny it. "That means destruction.
If it's not a housing development, it'll be something else
equally as bad."

"Not all change is a bad thing," Alec reminded her.
"Sometimes it's for a good reason. It fulfills a need."

Shea swallowed uncomfortably. "And what about people
who like things as they are?"

"Change is part of life. Most people are willing to accept it if they understand the reasoning behind it, especially if it benefits them in some way. You're painting me
as the bad guy before you even know what my intentions
are for this place."

"Oh, I see." She looked at Alec. "I should let you take
over my ranch and trust you to develop it in a manner you
think is—"

"Shea, it's not *your* ranch!"

"The hell it's not!" she muttered.

"Then show me your name on a deed."

"How can you be so…two-faced? How could you talk
and laugh with the people there tonight, sit at their table,
share their food, all the while knowing what you plan to
do to their community if given the chance?"

"You make it sound like I intend to rob them!" Alec responded, his tone incredulous.

"Stab them in the back would be more accurate."

"For God's sake. You've got to be the most narrowminded, bullheaded woman I've ever come across in my life!"

"Well, as my grandfather used to say, that's the pot calling the kettle black."

He turned off the main road onto the winding driveway leading to the old farmhouse. As Alec swung into the parking space, Shea grabbed for the door handle and was out of the car before he could turn off the ignition. She walked through the kitchen, up the stairs and into the bedroom, slamming the door behind her.

Angrily, she paced the floor until, finally realizing the futility of the situation she changed her clothes, brushed her teeth, switched off the lights and climbed into bed. A few minutes later, Alec joined her, arranging his pillows but making no attempt to acknowledge her presence. He lay on his side facing away from her. Instead of being relieved, she was irritated, and that was crazy. She should be glad. But she wasn't and she refused to dwell on why.

The distant rumble of thunder shattered the serene silence, waking Alec from his sleep. The sky was still dark even though the clock on the nightstand said it was almost five in the morning. Faint flashes of lightning intermittently lit the room for a few brief seconds as the increasing winds surged around the corner of the old house. He immediately thought of Scotty. Steve would have both boys inside Leona's house by now. It was a new and comforting realization that he could leave his only child in the care of near strangers and trust, without any hesitation, that his son would be well taken care of. Such trust was almost unheard of in his world.

Alec started to turn over, but immediately felt a soft, warm body snuggled against him. The aura of innocence and trust as Shea slept was alien to him. Hell, everything about her, about this place, was so different than what he was used to. Yet, at the same time, it often felt as though he'd come home.

With his sexual frustration at its peak, his body ached with desire every time she came close and now was no exception. He didn't know how much strength remained before his good intentions would go out the window. He'd never have believed he could become this damned infatuated with anyone, especially after Sondra. With a groan of frustration, he eased Shea onto a pillow and got out of bed.

The few days he'd originally anticipated being here had rolled into weeks. He'd surprised himself by actually finding a way to continue his own work and still enjoy the physical labor the ranch required. Ironically, it was in that labor he found an inner peace. A fresh breeze on his face, sweet scents in the air and the sun on his back. Beat the hell out of any gym.

He pulled on some jeans and grabbed a shirt and his boots. He needed to put some space between himself and Shea. A lot of space. One last glance at the bed where she slept was all it took to confirm in his mind what his body had been telling him. He wanted her. Desperately. And the frazzled strength of the single thread of determination that held him at bay was about to snap.

Nine

By six o'clock the rainstorm was over and the morning dawned clear. The eastern sky lit up in glorious color, heralding the sun's imminent appearance. Alec threw the last of the coffee down his throat and turned away from the kitchen window, stepped outside and meandered toward the barn. As he got close, the scents of alfalfa and pine shavings permeated the air. Soft nickers greeted his approach, bringing a smile of contentment to his face.

Entering the barn, he followed the bank of stalls until he came to number twelve. The big bay gelding was licking the last remnants of breakfast from his feed trough.

"You're up mighty early."

He turned to see Hank amble in his direction.

Alec nodded.

"You want me to throw a saddle on him for you?" Hank asked.

He hadn't thought about going for a ride, but the idea immediately took hold and it was too perfect to pass up.

"I'll do it," Alec replied. "Where's the tack?"

A few minutes later, Alec rode the big horse out the main gate and headed north. Ransom was excited about the outing, dancing against the firm hold Alec kept on the reins. Hank had mentioned the old homestead and provided general directions. It sounded like the perfect place to think.

The rutted path eventually grew less and less visible as the big bay continued to carry him through the trees and

over the rolling hills. After an hour, Alec began to relax.
The serenity of the countryside, the wind blowing softly
through the leaves of the trees, helped clear his head. He
honestly loved it here. He again experienced a twinge of
regret over the changes that would soon come. For the first
time in his life, the jubilance of building something great
was overshadowed by the nagging uneasiness over the fact
that he was about to destroy something very special.

Not surprising, his thoughts turned to Shea. Her determination to keep this spread should be an obstacle to overcome, not something to admire. But that was before their
wedding night when she'd been so gut-wrenchingly beautiful and so damn sensual. It was before he'd seen her laugh,
before she'd received hugs from his usually standoffish son.
Before she'd shared her concerns about the ranch and had
begun to trust him enough to open up and talk to him about
things that troubled her. Before he'd seen her schoolgirl-
like grin over a bunch of silly wildflowers.

It was before she'd become someone special in his
life. Hell, they hadn't even had sex. But the longer he was
around her, the more he had to remind himself their marriage was based on a very bizarre two-hundred-year-old
contract. Becoming involved with Shea wasn't something
that should happen. But his gut instinct told him it was too
late. He'd already crossed that line.

Shea sat alone in the kitchen watching the morning unfold. She fixed a piece of dry toast, poured a cup of the
not-too-old coffee and decided she could afford to take the
time to enjoy part of the day. It was only five weeks until
fall roundup but all of the preparations had been made, the
equipment checked and ready to be taken to the site.

After clearing away the few dishes, she set off in the direction of the barn. Finding it empty, she walked down the
main hall toward Hank's house. As soon as she rounded

the corner, she saw him sitting on the wooden porch, leaning against a post with a wide-eyed little boy hanging on his every word. Apparently Hank had picked up the boy from his overnight stay at Leona's and from the lingering smell, they'd already enjoyed a breakfast of bacon and eggs.

"...So he lays real quiet-like and crawls on his belly—*real* slow—over to the fallen log. But just as he reaches fer his gun, this old owl comes screeching out of the trees and swoops down right at him."

"Wow..." Scotty's voice held the excitement of the moment. "What did he do?"

"Well, Roy reckons that old owl done give away his hiding place, don't ya see, so he pulls his gun from the holster, counts to three, then jumps out from behind the log with his gun a blazin'. Old Treach figured that owl was after a mouse so he never knew what hit him."

"Boom! Bang! He shot him! Didn't he, Hank?"

"He did fer a fact. Got the reward of all that gold and built him a little cabin right there on the bank of that river. Some people say his ghost still walks along the riverbank to this very day, protecting his gold."

"I wouldn't never go there 'cause he might think I was gonna steal it and I sure wouldn't want him to shoot at *me*!" Scotty shook his head, speaking in whispered excitement. Then he noticed Shea for the first time. "Did you ever see him? Old Roy?"

"Once. When I was about your age." She smiled and winked at Hank.

"Man..."

"How was your campout?"

"It was good!" Scotty answered, his eyes full of excitement. "We got hot dogs and cooked marshmallows on a stick. Mine got on fire."

"You had a campfire?"

"Uh-huh. And we heard the owl way deep in the woods.

Then we hadda go in the house cause of the rain. But it was *cool*."

Smiling, Shea turned her attention to Hank. "Where's Alec?"

"Said he was going to ride out to the north and see if he could find the old original homestead. Left here a couple of hours ago."

"Ride out…on what? You mean on a horse?"

"He saddled Ransom."

"Ransom!" He'd never make it back in one piece. Shea was incredulous. "And you let him? That horse could—"

"He's a big boy, Shea." Hank squinted up at her. "I watched him saddle the gelding and swing up like he'd been doing it all his life. Didn't seem to have any problem with him." He shrugged and bent his head, his attention focused on the small stick he'd been whittling.

Alec told her it had been a long time since he'd been on a horse. To handle Ransom as proficiently as Hank described, he would have to be a skillful horseman. A feeling of unease ran down her spine. She turned and quickly made her way back into the barn.

The stalls were empty. Hank must have moved the horses to the other barn in preparation for the drive. She marched straight down the main hall and back toward the house. Her truck was missing. She supposed Jason or one of the other hands had borrowed it, which wasn't unusual. She didn't see Alec's car either, which *was* unusual. Maybe Alec had let one of the hands use it to run into town. It wouldn't be the first time. She climbed into the only remaining vehicle in sight, the old white Jeep.

She wouldn't sit around and wait for Alec to come back. Something could happen. It was of equal concern that he was nosing around the old home site. It was a sacred place to her. She put the Jeep into gear and headed toward the big gate that opened to the northern pastures.

It was a bright, sunny day with not a cloud in the sky. All indications of the thunderstorms that had blanketed the area in the predawn hours were gone. Thanks to all the rain they'd had this spring, the grass was a deep, rich green. Shea should have enjoyed the outing. The old home site was her favorite place where the world couldn't come crashing in. It was a special place. A private place. Why had Alec headed there? With a grimace, she punched the pedal, and the Jeep bounced along the dwindling path into the deepening timber.

The trail cut through the forested area for several miles, skirting the vast grasslands to the west. It wound its way through the trees, over a rise and down into a small valley. The cooling waters of a small lake glistened in the sun as a gentle breeze sent small waves to lap against the shore. It was just past this tranquil setting that one would find traces of the original home site.

Shea shifted to a lower gear as the vehicle climbed the rise past the lake. As she topped the hill, she spotted Ransom, his front feet tethered, contentedly munching the tender, knee-high grass.

Pulling up a short distance away from the remains of the old foundation, she killed the motor and stood up in the seat. Immediately, she became aware of the silence. Somewhere in the distance, a meadowlark sang. The trees, touched by the gentle breeze, danced to its song.

Leaving the Jeep, she walked purposefully in the direction of the old home. There was very little left of the original structure. Not surprising since fire had raged through the timbers, followed by the ravages of the elements for two hundred years. The giant cinder blocks supporting the foot-thick oak timbers and roughly hewn floorboards were still intact. Three walls, log and mortar, and a corner of the original lower roof remained, their edges bearing traces of the fire that had claimed the house. The tall, sturdy chimney rose impressively as if daring anyone to challenge its right to be there.

"It's incredible." Alec's deep voice beckoned from behind her. Shea spun around, watching him casually walk toward her.

"Yes," she replied warily. "Is this where you're going to build your shopping mall?"

Alec ignored her taunt. He looked at the ancient dwelling. "Tell me about the house. Did they bring in the logs or were there trees this size on the land?" He looked up at the remaining roof.

"The logs for the house were all cut from here. The stones used in both the chimney and for some of the floor support were gathered from the creek bed." Shea pointed to the east. "Down there." Alec nodded, silently encouraging her to continue.

"The house had only two rooms and a loft. The kitchen was separate, over there." She nodded in the direction of the far side of the structure. "It used to have a covered breezeway linking it to the house. You can still see some of its foundation."

"What happened?"

She shrugged. "I'm not sure exactly what caused the fire. Dad tried to find out once, but there were no records. He believed lightning struck the roof. I think he said that someone died. There wasn't a lot anyone could do to save the structure. The remains you see here are probably thanks to a few buckets of water from the well."

"So, after the fire, your family rebuilt in the present location?"

"Yeah." Shea pushed away a strand of hair the wind had blown in her face as she looked at him with curiosity. "Why are you so interested? I mean, what does any of this matter to you?"

Alec turned away, looking out over the surrounding area.

"If you'll remember, it was my ancestors' land. They lived here, too."

She couldn't argue with that. He had as much a right to seek his heritage as she did.

"Behind the house—" she pointed west "—on top of the far rise is the old family cemetery. I think one of your relatives might be there, as well."

"I'd like to see."

Together they walked to the small burial ground. The names and dates on the long-standing headstones were partially obscured, some more than others. The men and women who had come to this land, driven by a desire to build a future and the courage to tame the raw wilderness, now rested in peace on this small patch of earth. At the edge of the area, two headstones stood slightly apart from the others.

Alec read one of them. "'William Alec Morreston. Born 1780. Died 1848.' My great-great-grandfather."

Shea reached out and gently touched William's stone. "Odd he was buried here. He was originally from the north, wasn't he?"

"Yeah." Alec nodded. "My grandmother used to tell me stories of how her grandfather loved the West. He came out here as a young man and fell in love with this part of the country. There was a young woman he met here. Alyssa, I think. He wrote that they were to be married, but she died before it could happen. Eventually, he returned to the family home in New York but I guess this is where he wanted to be laid to rest."

"At least someone in your family had some sense," Shea couldn't resist saying. She glanced at Alec in time to see a grin pull at the corners of his mouth.

"I have some old letters indicating he was a trapper. He used the river for his transportation and supposedly built a cabin, probably more of a shack, not far from here. Does the property reach as far as the river?"

She nodded. "Yeah. About a mile in that direction."

"You up for a hike?"

"We could take the Jeep."

"Let's go."

It took only a few minutes to reach the river's edge. Together, they walked along the high riverbank looking out over the wide expanse of the Red River. Appropriately named—the red clay, seen in the shallow parts of the riverbed and in the steep canyon walls flanking each side, cast a pinkish glow in the late afternoon sun.

"I don't think I'm going to find anything." He stood, hands resting on his hips, gazing out over the scenic terrain. "I'm sure the river has changed its banks dramatically in the last two hundred years. Erosion probably destroyed any remnants long ago." He sounded regretful.

"You're probably right, but it never hurts to look."

Alec's interest in his heritage surprised her. The questions he'd asked about the Hardin home site and now the interest in his own ancestral home didn't fit the image of the modern builder who wanted to level everything. She couldn't stop from watching him as he continued looking out over the scenic waterway. From his tawny eyes and full lips to the strong, deep set of his jaw, his face was temptation run amuck. Add intelligence sprinkled with a sense of humor, and it all added up to an irresistible combination.

In a moment of clarity, she realized she had come to respect Alec. He was a successful businessman and builder, a great father and a man of his word. But the reason he was here sent a twinge of sadness inching its way to her heart.

At that moment, he turned toward her and she made the mistake of looking into his eyes. The smile faded and his eyes darkened to the color of molten topaz. She knew he saw the awareness in her face. She swallowed hard.

The cry of a hawk circling overhead broke the spell.

"It's getting late. The sun has almost set. We'd better get back," she whispered, turning away.

In silent agreement they climbed into the Jeep and headed back to the home site and the trail leading home.

Ransom was still contentedly munching on the knee-high grass when the Jeep pulled up near the old homestead. Alec approached the big gelding and ran his hand down the glossy neck, then looked at the last rays of the setting sun in the open western sky.

"Is it true a horse can find his way back home on his own?"

Shea pursed her lips to hide a grin, nodding. "They usually know where the food is. Go ahead and unsaddle him and turn him loose. You can ride back in the Jeep. We wouldn't want Scotty to think his dad doesn't know which way is up in the dark."

"Ha. Ha."

With the saddle, bridle and tether removed, Ransom acknowledged his freedom by kicking his heels in the air and running for home, his tail held high above his back. Alec put the tack in the Jeep and climbed into the passenger seat. She slid in behind the wheel and turned the key. The engine caught, but immediately sputtered and died. She tried again, but it refused to start. Pumping the gas pedal did no good either.

"Mind if I have a try?" They switched places, but Alec had no more luck getting it started than she had. He walked to the front and opened the hood. "Everything looks okay," he muttered. "How much gas did you have?"

"I filled up last week and haven't really gone anywhere except over to Leona's. It should have plenty."

"Well, it doesn't." Alec closed the hood.

It was miles back to the ranch house. By the angle of the

sun, it would be dark in less than an hour. A quick glance revealed he was thinking the same thing.

He walked over to a small crevice, kicked at the grass, then looked out over the far hills as if deep in thought. He smiled, shook his head, then he began gathering rocks, placing them in a circle around the indention.

"Are you building a fire?"

"Yeah. It might get cold later tonight." He looked at her. "Unless you know of a better way we can keep warm?"

She ignored his teasing. "Hank will know something's wrong and come after us. You don't really need to do that."

Alec dropped more sticks into the circle. "It might be a while. Are there any matches in the Jeep?"

"Not that I've ever seen but I'll look." She walked to the front of the vehicle. Opening the glove box, she found not one, but two lighters and a small box of matches.

"I don't know how these got there, but here you go," she said, tossing him a lighter.

"How about water?"

"We don't keep water in the Jeep. If we're headed out to a branding or mending a long stretch of fence—something that will take a day or more—we load a couple of big ice chests and some ten-gallon coolers in the supply trailer and pull it to the site."

He nodded. "Would you humor me?"

With a shrug, Shea returned to the back of the vehicle. Moving aside Ransom's saddle and an old tarp, she immediately spotted two jugs of water. Frowning, she looked at Alec.

"And...?"

She pulled out the two gallons of water. "I don't understand—"

"It's just a guess, but I think Hank knew we would need matches and water before you ever left the ranch."

"What? What are you saying?"

"This." He gestured with his hands. "Our being out here alone…stranded. It was a setup. It was planned."

"No." Shea denied his words, but at the same time, her heart increased its rhythm. "Hank…wouldn't do something like that."

"Okay." He squatted next to the small pile of wood, tearing dried grass and shoving it underneath the smaller sticks.

"I've known him all my life. He just isn't the kind of person to…to…"

"Play matchmaker?"

"Exactly."

"Take a look in the back. I'm betting you'll find some blankets. While you're there, you might check and see what we're having for dinner."

Shea opened her mouth to argue but closed it again without a word. She set the containers of water on the ground and turned back to the Jeep. Partially hidden farther under the tarp were a sleeping bag, two pillows, a couple of blankets and a small ice chest. A thermos and a few foam cups completed the stash.

"I don't know of anyone else who would drain the gas tank and load the Jeep with supplies two people would need for a night," Alec said, walking over to where she stood. "Do you?"

She was dumbfounded that Hank Minton, of all people, would do this. But it could be no one else. "No." When she got back to the ranch, he was going to get a piece of her mind.

Shea watched the last of the sun's glow surrender to the multitude of stars in the night sky. The wood in Alec's campfire popped and hissed as the flames danced over the dried branches, releasing the tantalizing aroma of hickory and pecan into the still night air.

They ate in companionable silence. The sandwiches in

the small ice chest went quickly, along with the slices of apple pie and coffee.

Finally, unable to hold any more, she dropped the remains of her meal into the baggie. Leaning back against a big rock, she stretched out her legs and pulled the blanket around her shoulders. The temperature had begun to drop as the sun disappeared.

"Want another cup of coffee?" Alec sat next to her, his arms resting on his knees as he, too, looked up at the night sky.

"No, thanks." She leaned her head back against the boulder. "I still can't believe Hank set us up."

"He's from the old school," Alec replied. "Married people don't live separately. They don't argue all the time—"

"They don't leave their wife the morning after the wedding."

"And the wife damn sure doesn't spend her wedding night in the barn."

"You're right," she murmured. "Hank did it."

"I'll bet he had help."

She turned to look at him. "What do you mean? Who?"

"A couple of nights ago, when I tucked him in, Scotty voiced some concern about having to leave here. I hadn't said anything about him returning to New York, and I didn't understand what would cause him to worry about it. He must have figured if we didn't get along—"

"Then he'd have to leave." Shea finished the thought. "Set up by a four-year-old."

"He's smart, capable of a lot more than you'd expect for his age," Alec replied. "Which is another reason I wanted him here with me." He chuckled. "He's run off two nannies so far and his grandmother is on her last nerve, even though she would never admit it."

"Hank mentioned he's been asking about a horse."

"I know," Alec replied. "He's talked about little else since he got here."

"Alec, I'm hesitant to mention this because I still worry over Scotty's safety, but we have a gelding. Been around here forever," she ventured. "He's a small horse, older than I am, and as gentle as they come. He loves people. If you want Scotty to learn to ride, he couldn't be any safer than on Marty. I think Scotty would like him. He's a paint and kinda flashy."

Alec appeared to consider the suggestion. He glanced toward her, grinned and nodded his approval. "I appreciate your offer. I think that would be great."

For a while they sat back listening to the fire crackle. Somewhere out in the woods a pack of coyotes made its presence known.

"Alec, I…I never asked if there was someone special in your life. I mean, it's a little late now, but—"

"No." Alec shook his head. "No one special."

"But you were married…?" she prompted, hating herself for showing any interest at all, but unable to contain her curiosity.

"Yes. I was married. For just over a year." Alec hesitated, as if debating whether to say anything else. Finally, he said, "It wouldn't have lasted that long if she hadn't gotten pregnant. Scotty was the only good thing to come out of it."

He was quiet for a few minutes. "It didn't take her long after we married to realize the role of wife and mother was not for her. I never knew about the other man until after she'd walked out. For whatever reason, she decided to go through with the pregnancy. For nine months, I lived with the possibility that the baby wasn't mine. Then one day, I came home to find a stranger standing outside my door with a baby in her arms. She handed him to me and said he was my son. My ex didn't even bring Scotty to me herself.

After that I heard she started partying pretty good. A few months later, she was dead of an overdose."

"Oh, my gosh! Alec. How horrible. I'm so sorry."

He shrugged as though it was nothing, but Shea sensed it had affected him deeply. It must be a terrible thing to find out the person you love had betrayed you. Alec deserved respect for raising his son alone, giving the baby all the love he needed. Scotty was proof positive Alec was a great dad.

"What about you?" he asked. "Any broken hearts because of this situation?"

The image of David's face popped into her mind, and she couldn't help but wonder what course his life had taken. It couldn't possibly be as bizarre as the direction hers had gone.

"No."

"I find that hard to believe."

Shea shrugged. "There was a guy in college. He was the one who called the night we were married. Haven't seen him in a long time but he's still a good friend. We talked about getting married but we both knew it wouldn't work. We wanted different things out of life. Then Dad got sick. I left school to take care of him and run the ranch. There was just never any time for…anything else."

"What was your major?"

"Veterinary medicine."

"You're a vet?"

She shook her head. "No. I got as far as my master's. That's when Dad became ill, so I came home. I'd hoped to have a practice someday. But things don't always work out like you plan." She shook herself out of somber thoughts that would serve no purpose and smiled at Alec. "Do you have any other family? I mean, besides Scotty?"

"One brother, Mike. And my mother lives with her sister in St. Petersburg, Florida."

"Do they know you're married?"

"No. I wrestled with the idea, but didn't exactly know how to explain our situation."

Shea nodded her understanding. "What's your mom like?"

Alec appeared to think on that for a while. "My mother. How do I describe my mother?" He shook his head. "She's a character. As hardheaded as you are." He shot her a grin. "In fact, the two of you together could make a guy absolutely crazy. She's smart, good-natured, has a terrific sense of humor, but she also has a strength. After my father died, she kept me in school and had the patience of a saint. I have her to thank for where I am today."

She sounded like someone Shea would love to meet, but sadly that probably would never happen. She now understood where Alec got his dogged determination. It also was obvious he loved his mother very much. Apparently they had a close relationship. Alec was, indeed, like an onion, and with every layer Shea peeled away, the more exceptional he became.

He was not a cold, heartless adversary as she'd initially thought. He was a man who respected family values. And despite the situation over the land, he had a good heart. In fact, she couldn't imagine herself ever finding a man better suited to her and to this life.

And that realization was very unsettling.

"I'm hesitant to bring this up," Alec remarked, absently dragging a small stick over the ground. "I keep waiting for a good time to mention it, but…I doubt if such a time exists."

Shea's heart missed a beat. There was only one thing he would be so hesitant to mention. The future of the Bar H. "Well, you have my curiosity roused. Go ahead." She forced a smile but refused to look at Alec.

"There's a meeting scheduled at the end of the month at a hotel in Dallas. All the investors will be there. Probably some of the local jurisdictions represented, as well. We're building a resort, Shea. Hotels, casinos, a theme park, some restaurants on the Oklahoma side. A water park, golf course and a couple more restaurants in Texas." He was quiet for a moment. "I'd like you to go with me to the meeting."

Shea immediately shook her head and swallowed the huge lump that formed in her throat. "That is not where I want to be."

"Shea, it's going to happen. The change is inevitable. You need to come to terms with the possibility that—" Alec stopped midsentence. "Look, maybe there's a way both of us can get what we want. Compromise might be a possibility. I'm open to trying, but you have to see the plans—with an open mind—then tell me if you think something can be worked out."

She looked above her to the millions of stars in the black velvet sky and shook her head at the hopelessness of her plight.

"So you think my cattle can skip the fall roundup and spend a few days at your resort?" She took in a deep breath. "We both know there is only one way this will end, Alec. One of us has to leave."

"So…you refuse to even try to see if there is an alternative." It was as much a statement as a question.

"I don't see how there could be."

"And you won't unless you attend the meeting. See for yourself." Alec tossed the small stick into the fire. "If I were in your place, I would want to learn everything I could about the enemy and their intent."

She shot him a look of surprise.

"Maybe," she finally agreed. *And maybe not.*

She heard him sigh. "It's late. We have a long walk in the morning. I suggest we bed down in the corner of the old house." He stood and poured out the last drops of his coffee. "I don't care to wake up in the morning and find one of your country varmints in our bed."

While they'd been sharing a bed for some time there was something about sliding into a sleeping bag with Alec that screamed disaster. And she needed some time to come to grips with what he'd just told her. A large resort would be worse than a shopping mall. But she didn't have a clue what her friends and neighbors would think of such a thing.

"Do what you want. I'm sleeping in the Jeep," she said. "Take the bedroll. I'll be fine with the blanket."

His eyebrows rose in quiet speculation, but he said nothing as she retraced her steps to the Jeep. It took some maneuvering, but she finally managed to shift around enough junk to make a reasonably sized sleeping space. She tossed him the bedroll and a pillow and climbed in.

"I heard rumblings of thunder earlier," Alec said. "There's no top on the Jeep. Are you sure you want to—"

"Yes, I'm sure," she quickly assured him. The whole day had been bright and sunny without a cloud in the sky. How gullible did he think she was?

She settled under the warm folds of the blanket and tried to get comfortable in the tiny space. By the time the first rays of the sun broke over the distant hills, she would be halfway back to the house.

And the first thing on her to-do list when she got there was find Hank Minton.

And maybe start looking for another place to live.

Ten

The uncomfortable sensation of cold water running across her face and down her neck woke her from a sound sleep. Brushing the moisture away with her hand, she blinked her eyes and pushed into a sitting position. It was dark. So incredibly dark she couldn't see her hand in front of her face. And it was raining—gently, but steadily. As she came fully awake, she noted the blanket was drenched, as were her clothes.

Muttering to herself, she climbed out of the Jeep. The wind had picked up, dropping the temperature, and she shivered as she stumbled in the direction of the homestead and what shelter it offered. The dying embers of the campfire provided just enough light to see the last few steps.

As she approached the old log structure, the skies opened up in a downburst. Climbing onto the floorboards, she followed the wall of the building to the back of the structure where a section of the roof remained.

"Over here." Alec spoke from the darkness.

Cautiously she followed the direction of his voice until her toes found the edge of the sleeping bag. Squatting down, she felt for the edge of the bedroll.

"Here," Alec said, and suddenly his hand held hers. "Shea, you're soaked. Get out of those clothes. Don't argue."

Teeth chattering, she unbuckled her belt, unzipped the wet denim and struggled to push her jeans down her legs. Finally, Alec grabbed the end of the legs, and with one hard tug, she was free of the soggy pants. She scooted inside the soft fleece lining, still warm from the heat of his body.

"And the shirt," he said, not bothering to wait for an argument. He efficiently pulled it over her head, tossed it away and lay down next to her. His heavy arms wrapped around her and their legs entwined, as he began rubbing her arm and shoulder, the friction bringing much-needed warmth.

"No 'I-told-you-so's?'"

"Not this time."

The rain surged, pelting the wooden roof above them. The moist air carried the heavy scent of pine, and in the distance a lone coyote called out to its kinsmen. Alec's hands eventually stilled and merely held her next to the warmth of his body.

Her mind whirled, preventing the return of sleep. Alec was as complex as a jigsaw puzzle whose pieces were upside down. One minute he came off as hard and unrelenting, but the next minute he lay in the shelter of a centuries-old, burned-out building, holding her in his arms, ready to protect her from whatever might be out there. And he seemed completely comfortable in either role.

In fairness, she had to question her own sanity. Here she lay in the home of her ancestors, the last surviving heir, held warm and protected in the arms of the enemy, the very man who would destroy it all.

The low, rumbling thunder gradually became louder, the flashes of lightning brighter. Alec lay in the black shadows, holding Shea as she slept. Lowering his head, he breathed in the sweet scent of her hair.

A long, increasingly loud rumble of thunder was followed by more flashes of light. Shea turned her face into his neck and covered her ears with her hands.

"Shea?"

"The storm."

"It's all right, hon." He tried to soothe her.

"I hate storms. Please try to start the Jeep again." Her voice was high, frightened, her words partially muffled by his shoulder.

"It doesn't have any gas, remember?" His arms resumed their circular motion on her back. "We'll be all right. This old house has weathered more bad weather than you and I will ever see."

Another loud crack of thunder shook the floor. She raised her head and, through the flashes of light from the storm, he saw the fear in the blue iridescence of her eyes. Her sensuous lips parted slightly and desire charged through his body like a bolt of the lightning from above.

Slowly, she reached out and placed her hand against the side of his face as if making certain he was there. He didn't move, didn't breathe, afraid that doing so would break the spell that held them. She leaned forward, moistening his lips with her tongue before kissing him fully. The blood pounded in his head, surged straight to his groin.

He responded without thinking as passion flared. He didn't know if she actually wanted him or if she was half-asleep and didn't realize what she was doing. But whatever the reason, she didn't pull away. And despite his earlier resolve, neither could he.

With a last surge of willpower, he set her away from him.

"Alec?"

"Shea, listen to me." His voice was rough, even to his own ears. "I can't do this anymore. It's no longer a game. All bets are off. If you don't want me to make love to you, then move away. Now."

In the ensuing silence, he assumed she realized how close she'd come to losing her resolve, that there would be no turning back. The bedroll moved as she shifted her body. But instead of turning away, she kissed his chest, her teeth nipping his skin, her tongue tasting his heated flesh.

Like a man driven by forces beyond his control, he pushed her fully onto her back, pressed her down into the thick bedroll. Warm and pliant, her flesh conformed to his like the rain that filled each tiny crevice of the parched earth.

In that moment, he knew it was no longer a bluff to get her to leave. She was his wife, regardless of the circumstances. And he wanted her. Oh, how he wanted her. He needed to feel his hard flesh sheathed inside. She was his. And he'd make damn sure she knew it. His mouth found hers, plunging his tongue inside, loving the taste of her, the feel of her. And this time Shea kissed him back.

With a moan of defeat, Alec kissed her deeply, urgently, with a hunger that threatened to consume him. He heard her whimper, and the blood pounded in his ears. His hand followed the exquisite contours of her body, cupping her perfect breast, his thumb teasing the taut nipple. He left her lips, kissing down her throat to the supple flesh he held in his hand, teasing the small nub. She arched her back, pushing her chest toward him with a soft moan and he gave equal attention to her other perfect breast. With his hand, he traced over her belly, then lower to the silken curls that framed the center of her desire.

"Alec," she whispered, need heavy in her voice as she pushed against his hand.

The pain in his loins became unbearable as raw, primitive instinct took over.

He moved fully on top of her and she opened to him. His hand fisted her hair, drawing her head back, allowing him greater access to her mouth, and like a starving man, he fed.

Alec raised his head and through the flashes of radiant light, he looked into the blue iridescent depths of her eyes and with a hoarse, almost feral growl, he pushed inside.

The thunder rolled, escalating in power, mirroring the intensity of their joining. Shea struggled to accept him, her body stretching as his power filled her. She knew no fear of the storm. Her mind and body were consumed with Alec, all senses tuned to him. She could no longer think. Only feel. And the feeling was incredible. Every movement of his big, powerful body propelled her higher. Her arms slid up and over his broad shoulders to circle his neck, her fingers gripped his thick hair.

Alec's lips returned to hers, his tongue pushing deep. His hands cupped her head, holding her where he wanted her to be and a pressure inside began to build, causing a need that was almost painful in its intensity.

"Alec!" she cried out against his lips.

"I know, babe. Let it happen."

Rotating his hips, he pushed hard and suddenly her desire crested and her mind shattered into a million brilliant pieces. She cried out his name as wave after wave of complete and total fulfillment coursed through her body.

He kissed her again with animal hunger. He began to move with a driving force, bringing her to the edge of mindless release for a second time. She clutched at his broad shoulders as his hands moved to cup her hips, lifting her, filling her, until, with a wild growl, he reached the summit of his own release. He shuddered against her as the spasms of his completion vibrated through him, and pushed her over the top yet again.

Spent, he collapsed on top of her. His heavy weight made it difficult to breathe, but she never would have asked him to move away. Surrounded by his musky scent she could feel the rapid beating of his heart. Wrapped in the warmth and protection of his arms, she floated slowly back to earth. Outside their shelter the rain continued to fall.

It was as though neither of them was inclined to move for fear they would somehow lose this sweet accord, this exquisite joining of their bodies and souls. She wanted this moment to go on, for him to hold her like this forever.

Rising up on his arms, his eyes captured hers, his thumb gently tracing the contours of her lips. In those moments, time stood still.

Finally, he eased from her but held her close.

"Did I hurt you?" he asked, bringing her hand to his lips.

"No." She smiled and gently touched his face.

She knew the pain would come later.

When this situation was over and Alec said goodbye.

"Shea—" Alec's voice called to her, bringing her back from the blissful realm of sleep. "Shea, hon, wake up."

She moaned her disgruntlement and attempted to snuggle back into the heavenly cocoon of their soft makeshift bed.

"Come on, sweetheart." Alec kissed her before pulling the warmth of the bedroll away from her. "I think we're about to have company."

Before she could respond, a piercing light shattered the darkness, followed by the sound of an engine and tires bouncing through the small pools of water in the rain-drenched earth.

Struggling to sit up, she pulled the top of the sleeping bag around her. "What is it?"

"I think we're being rescued."

"Rescued? What time is it?" The rain had slowed to a drizzle, but the sky was still black.

"Just after midnight."

"You both all right in there?" Hank's voice called from the truck as he pulled up in front of the foundation. "Got kinda worried when the storm broke. Figured I'd better come out and check."

Her eyes locked to Alec's, she didn't immediately move.

Then, with a grimace, he rolled onto his side and reached for his jeans.

Shea found the blanket he'd been using, pulled it around her, gathered her wet clothes and stood up. Hank's arrival had effectively melted away the sweet fantasy and slammed her back to reality.

What had she done?

She didn't look in Alec's direction as she walked toward Hank and the truck.

The trip back was made in silence, her earlier intentions to wring Hank's neck now overshadowed by confusion. She must be crazy. How could she have made love with the man who threatened to take away her ranch and everything she cherished?

A slight tremble ran down her spine and she pulled the blanket more tightly around her. Alec reached out and turned up the heater. But it wasn't the temperature in the truck's cab making her feel chilled to the bone.

Entering the house, she went straight upstairs. Maybe, with any luck she could be in bed and feign sleep when he got there. She quickly grabbed a clean T-shirt and panties, entered the bathroom and turned on the shower. Stepping under the spray, she leaned forward, placing her forehead against the shower wall, and let the hot water stream down her back.

Had she been wrong in making love to Alec? She didn't love him. She couldn't. She *wouldn't* fall in love with him. It had been hormones. Or the rain. Or momentary insanity. She gritted her teeth. This would only make everything worse.

Shower finished, she dressed for bed and pulled open the bathroom door. Alec stood in front of her, very tall, very imposing and very male. He was clad only in a towel slung low around his hips. He must have showered in the bathroom downstairs. He watched her with those cat eyes, alert to the emotions she tried to hide.

She forced a smile and moved to step around him. He caught her arm as she passed, gently halting her forward motion.

"Do we need to talk?"

She kept her vision focused on the floor. She didn't want to see the mockery in his eyes or the smirk that would be back on his face. "No."

He placed a finger under her chin, forced her to look into his eyes. Her gaze dropped lower, to his mouth, full, defined and capable of so much passion. There was no mockery. No contempt. No smirk.

"I disagree. I just made love to my wife, and now she doesn't want anything to do with me." He watched her intently, his head tilted in question. "I'd like to know why."

She shrugged. "I… It's awkward, Alec. For me. I mean, I'm not sure—"

"Where we go from here?"

She nodded. "Yeah."

He moved forward, resting his hands against the wall, his well-muscled biceps on either side of her head, and leaned down to her. "I say we take it one day at a time." His raspy voice was deep and wonderfully disturbing. He moved to her neck, nipped at the sensitive skin just below her ear. "I can't tell you I'll call off the project," he murmured, his breath hot against her skin. "There is already too much time and money invested and too many people involved," he murmured before moving to the other side of her neck and repeating the wildly arousing little bites. "But there has to be a way to work this out."

Every nip sent tingles of hot current jolting through her. He was doing it again. He was seducing her with his touch and his voice. Oh, how she wished they'd come together under different circumstances. But right then, she couldn't quite remember why it mattered.

"But for now I see no other immediate changes that are required." The look on his face told her he was serious.

As they stood in the shadows with his face so close she could touch her lips to his with minimal movement, the concern over the ranch faded somewhat. Yet she knew the only thing they'd truly accomplished was admitting their mutual desire for each other.

Mutely, she nodded, and his mouth came down over hers. The stubble of his beard scratched her skin, but she didn't care. God help her, at this moment she didn't care.

With a barely concealed moan, Alec scooped her into his arms and carried her to their bedroom, kicking the door closed behind them.

Eleven

The distant rumbling of thunder announced the approach of yet another summer storm. The humidity was high, the air thick. Alec found Shea in Scotty's bedroom, opening a window to allow the gentle breeze to penetrate the room's stuffiness.

"Does it always rain this much in Texas?" he asked from the doorway.

"Summer showers," she replied, turning to smile at him. "By mid-August we'll be wishing for some of this rain."

"Hey, Dad! Look what I won at the fair!" Scotty ran into the room fresh from his bath. Just after breakfast, Hank had taken him and Cody for a day at the county fair, giving Alec and Shea the entire day together without distractions. They hadn't wasted a second.

Scotty proudly grabbed a huge stuffed owl from atop his dresser. The oval face, covered in gray feathers, framed two huge round eyes. "Isn't it cool? Cody just won a stuffed bear. Boy, I was lucky, wasn't I, Daddy?"

"You sure were, son," Alec replied, smiling at Scotty.

"And I got to ride with Hank on his horse in the parade, and we ate hot dogs with ketchup, and we got some of the candy they threw from the…uh…uh…" He looked at Shea.

"Floats," Shea supplied.

"Yeah, from the floats. Then we saw the biggest pig get a ribbon, and Leonard Mabry let me brush his goat." He actually stopped and took a breath. "It was cool, Dad."

Grinning, Alec leaned over and placed a kiss on his son's head, then rustled the soft hair. Shea turned down the covers of the small bed. "Okay, in you go, cowboy."

Scotty ran to the window and carefully placed the owl on the windowsill. "Hank said this old owl will bring me luck. I'm gonna set it here so it will see me when I ride Marty."

The day after they'd been stranded at the old ruins, Hank had introduced Scotty to his first horse. Marty had indeed been a perfect choice, moving slow and gentle as though he knew his young rider was just learning. After only an hour of simple instruction, Scotty had been off and riding, making endless circles around one of the larger corrals.

The boy turned and jumped into the center of the mattress with a squeal and a giggle. Alec smiled and leaned over to tuck in his young son for the night.

Shea slipped out of the room, giving father and son some bonding time. The wind had picked up, and the sheer draperies fluttered gently inside the master bedroom. Suddenly, the rain began to fall, pelting against the top of the house, falling in heavy sheets from the edges of the roof. She walked to the dresser and took out a soft cotton T-shirt in preparation for her shower.

Large hands came to rest on her shoulders, their grip a welcome deterrent against the rain's sudden chill. Alec's arms came around her, pulling her back against his chest. His chin rested on her head.

"Thank you," he said quietly.

"For what?" A quizzical frown covered her face as she turned to her husband.

"For all you do for Scotty. And for me." He grinned. "Or, maybe I should I say *to* me."

"Both are my pleasure." She beamed.

"Come here," Alec whispered, pulling her down onto the bed and settling himself next to her. He began unbuttoning her blouse.

"I would like to know the name of the idiot who invented buttons," he muttered. "And why my wife insists on wearing clothing with them on it."

"What would you have me do? Wear nothing but T-shirts?"

"You've got it partially right. Just leave off the T-shirt."

She laughed, and he leaned over and placed his lips on hers.

She was so focused on Alec at first she ignored the cool, wet sensation on her forehead. As the feeling persisted, it became an irritant, breaking her focus and causing her to push Alec away. She sat up and wiped at her temple, noting the moisture on her hand.

Before she could assimilate her thoughts, another drop of something cold and wet hit her head then trickled down her scalp underneath her hair.

"Shea, what's wrong?"

She swung her legs to the side of the bed as another droplet of water splattered onto her shoulder and ran down her arm. She sprang from the bed. "Oh…Alec, it's—"

At that moment, with a sickening groan, a section of the ceiling above the bed collapsed, sending a downpour of accumulated rainwater squarely onto Alec's head.

With a shriek, she scampered back from the bed as a flash of lightning illuminated the room. Startled, she took in Alec, sitting on the bed, his hands held ineffectively above his head as a river of water cascaded down.

"Cool!" Scotty called out as he opened their bedroom door, no doubt hearing the loud crash as well as her shriek. His eyes were wide at the spectacle in front of him. "Hey, Dad, can I—"

"No!" Alec didn't give him a chance to finish the question. "Go into the bathroom and get a towel," he barked as he rolled off the bed, sending Scotty running down the hall.

Shea stood to the side, staring incredulously at her husband, who appeared to be in shock. He placed his hands on his hips and stared up at the heavily dripping ceiling, a look of amazement on his features.

Shea clenched her fists in a weak effort to contain her amusement but lost the battle as a fit of giggles overpowered her and she gave in to a moment of full-fledged laughter. Scotty returned with the towel, his giggles joining hers at the sight of his father standing drenched beside the bed.

"It's not that damn funny," he growled, which brought an encore of laughter from both of them. Alec snatched the towel from his son's hands and began to blot his head and neck.

"Hey, Daddy, you want some soap?"

Shea clamped her hand over her mouth and turned away from Alec as she fought to restrain the laughter. Suddenly, she was hoisted up into his arms.

"You think it's so funny?"

Before she could answer, she was tossed through the air, landing with a splash on top of the completely soaked mattress. There were matching screams and giggles from Scotty as he came to rest on the bed next to her.

"Why? Why go to the trouble of checking the foundation of a house you only want to tear down?"

Shea watched as Alec checked the flashlights while he waited for Jason to arrive.

"Because I want to know that it's safe. Obviously we won't be moving out as quickly as I'd originally anticipated." He shot her a knowing glance, his lips pursed to subdue the grin. "As old as this place is, it could be a death trap. I'm not about to endanger Scott's life—or yours—by taking that chance."

"Well, I think you're making this bigger than it is. You're going to extremes."

"I don't care. There may not be anything holding this

house together but the paint and even that's beginning to crack. I'm going over every square inch. It obviously needs a new roof."

"Oh yeah? How can you tell?" They'd spent the night in her old room and while it was not as comfortable as their new bed, especially for a man of Alec's size, Shea had slept peacefully. The cold rainwater shower hadn't dampened his sexual appetite, and after they'd managed to get Scotty back to sleep, Alec had wasted no time proving it.

"Yeah, Daddy," Scotty chimed in. "How can you tell?" A quelling look from his father did little to silence his giggles, but he scooted out of his chair. "I'm gonna go see what Hank's doing."

"Breakfast will be ready in an hour," Shea called. "Tell Hank to have you back here by nine."

"Okay," he replied, as the door slammed behind him.

"This is serious, Shea," Alec said as he poured another cup of coffee. "How long has it been since this house was checked?"

"Checked for what?" She put the strips of bacon into the large iron skillet. The sizzle and aroma immediately filled the air.

"Wood rot. Termites. Faulty wiring. Leaking pipes. Any number of things."

She shrugged. "I really don't know."

"How long since the roof was replaced?"

She again shrugged her shoulders. "Dad always said he was going to have it repaired, but I don't think he ever got around to it. We've had some leaks from time to time, and the roof was patched in those areas." She'd hoped that would suffice until there was money for a new roof.

Alec grimaced. "Then you don't know how much water damage there's been?" Shea shook her head. "What about the foundation?"

"What about it?"

"How long since it's been examined?" He looked at Shea's blank expression. "Never mind. I think I can guess. There's been virtually no protective maintenance. In two hundred years. Amazing. I intend to find out exactly what's going on. I'm afraid the incident last night was only a hint of other problems."

Shea turned the bacon over in the pan and mentally crossed her fingers. If Alec found serious damage, she didn't know where she would get the money for the repairs.

When breakfast was over, Alec went to find Jason, impatient to get started. The two men took the soaked mattress downstairs, Alec still muttering about the roof as they went. Then he located a ladder, loaded two flashlights with fresh batteries and they were off. She knew Alec was more than qualified. Inspecting the house would be like child's play to him.

She called a local roofing company to come out and give an estimate on repairs. For the rest of the day, she stayed close to the house, finishing laundry, preparing a brisket and waiting for the arrival of the roofers.

A few minutes before Shea was about to call Alec and Scotty in for supper, Alec came into the kitchen. He was covered in dirt and grime from his head to his feet. A scowl was firmly in place.

"Give me a few minutes to get cleaned up," he said and walked toward the stairs.

A short time later, Alec reentered the kitchen.

"So, how bad is the roof?"

"It's not good."

"It can be repaired where it fell in and—"

"It's not just the roof, Shea," he cut in. "There's major wood rot and termite damage everywhere. I found extensive destruction to most of the load-bearing walls on the first floor, and the foundation is crumbling. The house has already begun to shift. Its ability to remain standing for much longer is highly questionable." He rubbed the back of his neck. "That aside, the wiring is sixty years old. The plumbing needs replacing, the gas line is highly suspect and I'd guess most of your heat during the winter flies out the old single-pane windows. Did you know several are cracked?"

"So, what are you saying?" She wanted him to spell it out. "If…if it's the cost, I could replace one thing at a time over the next few—"

"Shea, the house isn't safe." His words caused a sick feeling in the pit of her stomach. "We shouldn't even be inside right now. It's not safe for you—or any of us—to stay here. I don't know how much clearer I can make it."

She'd known the old house was long past need of repairs, but because the money wasn't there, she'd ignored the problems. Apparently, her father had done the same thing.

"So…what are my options?"

He shook his head. "The *only* option is tear it down and build a new one. But under the circumstances, that would be ridiculous."

Under the circumstances?

Her mind whirled, not wanting to believe what that meant. Was this his way of telling her it was over? She'd thought they had found something special between them. They made love every night. She'd even begun to believe the marriage was real—or had a chance to become so. Had he been plotting all along? Looking for a bona fide reason to make her leave?

Had he only been pretending he cared for her? If she'd been wrong to start trusting him…if he had only been using her while he waited for an opportunity that would allow him to reclaim the land, she didn't know how she would ever deal with that. She felt her heart drop to her knees as that possibility threatened to knock her off her feet.

She'd let herself believe he cared about her as well as the land. She'd let down her guard. Reality and disappointment hit with the force of a sledgehammer. With her pulse slamming through her veins, she removed the rolls from the oven, set the tray on top of the stove and stared at him. Suddenly it was overwhelming. The news about the house was bad enough. Her life was here, her past as well as her envisioned future rested on this small piece of earth. Everything she knew revolved around this ranch. She had nowhere else to go. Tears burned the backs of her eyes; her breath died in her throat.

But to think she would lose Alec as well, that she'd merely been used to relieve his boredom, that she meant nothing to him. How was she ever going to come to terms with that?

"Shea?"

Covering her mouth with her hand to try to muffle a cry of despair, she ran from the room as the tears spilled over.

Curling up on the end of the old bedraggled sofa in the den, she faced the worn recliner that sat in the corner of the room. Her father's chair. She could visualize him kicked back, his feet resting on the stool as he read his afternoon paper. He was gone now. This house was the only connection she had to him and to her mother. Every room, every space under its roof carried precious memories. She could feel the love from the generations of family who had lived here before. Her dad's boots still sat in a corner of the mudroom. Her grandmother's handmade quilts were spread over the beds upstairs. It was as if the house gave her the strength to carry on alone. It was unthinkable that she had failed to protect it.

"Shea?" Alec entered the room. He stood just inside the open doorway, his hands resting on his hips.

She didn't want to talk with him. She couldn't. He might confirm that she was right in suspecting him.

"In the morning, you need to pack some clothes. I'll

make arrangements for us to stay in a hotel in Dallas for a while."

"And then what?" She gazed at her hands clenched tightly in her lap. "What happens next, Alec?"

"That's something we need to talk about. But regardless of what you decide to do going forward, staying here is not an option." He moved farther inside the room. "I'll still keep the promise I made that day in Ben's office. My original offer still stands. I'll buy you out. You can go back to school, get your doctorate and become a veterinarian. Fulfill that dream. You don't have to live here to do it. You need to be reasonable."

"Reasonable? Define reasonable. Is it unreasonable to want to stay in a place you love? A place you've based all your plans for a future around?"

"Maybe it's time for a change. Perhaps you should consider—"

"No." She shook her head defiantly. "No! Alec, you don't understand. I'm telling you I will not let this house be destroyed. Where would I go?"

"Anywhere you wanted."

"*Here* is where I want to be." *With you.*

Alec nodded, then shrugged. "Then you and your world will fall apart together. But I'll have no part of it."

Obviously, she'd been wrong when she'd assumed he cared about his ancestors, those who had so loved this land. The day they'd roamed around the old homestead and he'd asked all the questions. He'd wanted to see where his great-great-grandfather had been laid to rest. He'd commented that the area, the old cabin, were incredible. He'd shown what had appeared to be genuine interest. Had it all been a ploy to make her think he cared?

Had there ever been anything between them other than sex? She'd fallen in love with Alec, but he'd never said he felt the same. She swallowed hard as that realization hit.

Total humiliation washed over her, followed by a heightened sense of anger at herself for being so stupid. So gullible. Alec didn't love her. He never would. How could she have become so delusional as to believe a man like Alec Morreston would want any kind of permanent relationship with her?

She stood to face him. "I will not leave this house. You think you've won, but you haven't."

He reeled back as if she had slapped him. For a moment she thought she saw pain in his eyes, but it was gone so fast she knew she must have imagined it. The devil didn't have feelings.

"Won? Is that what you think this is about? Winning?"

She refused to answer. She knew what it was about and it wasn't their relationship. There was no relationship. There never had been. She'd played into his hands. He knew it and now so did she.

"If that's what you think, there's nothing more to say."

She walked to a nearby table, pulled a couple of tissues from the box. Wiping her eyes, she took a deep breath, struggling to control the pain running rampant through her body. She'd fallen in love with Alec, so much so she would have given him anything. But his only concern was getting her to vacate the property.

Suddenly, he was in front of her, his hands clutching her upper arms. His face was set in stone, his eyes narrowed. She could clearly detect the underlying thread of exasperation bordering on fury. "You're going to listen to me," he told her. "Tomorrow, you are going to start packing your bags because we are leaving this place—all of us."

"I'm not going anywhere—"

"And you're going to face the reality that life as you've known it is over. It's finished."

"No." She struggled, but he easily held her.

"Shea, stop! Listen to yourself. Take off the damn blinders and look at the truth that's right in front of you."

All she saw standing in front of her was the man she'd fallen in love with. A man who didn't love her, didn't care about anything but making more money. A man who'd done whatever was required to regain the land. Her first impressions had been correct. He was ruthless. She'd just never imagined how truly merciless he could be.

He turned and walked toward the door. "I had hoped that…" He shoved his hands into his jeans pockets and clenched his teeth. "I'm going to contact a building inspector. If you won't believe me, you can hear it from him. And I'm going to call the county. This house needs to be condemned."

She winced.

He paused at the door, his tawny eyes narrow and forbidding. "I'll have my jet readied for takeoff by tomorrow. I'm taking Scott back to New York. I'd like you to come with us, but that's your choice."

What would I do in New York?

The man who stood before her was ruthless and determined, powerful and unyielding, with the money and the resources to back him up. How could she ever have been so foolish as to think she could challenge him and win? What had she been thinking to let down her guard and start caring for him? It was no longer an either-or situation; the goal of winning Alec and the land had become one in the same. With the old house condemned, Alec would be gone, as well.

"I hate you for this." Her voice was low and broken. She gripped the back of the sofa to remain standing. It was a poor attempt to place armor around her heart. The words, like a boomerang, came right back at her, cutting deeply.

The hands of time stopped as they silently faced each other. Then Alec turned and walked out the door. She heard his footsteps going up the stairs and toward Scotty's bedroom, leaving Shea in the center of a room spinning wildly out of control. The searing pain in her chest made her gasp for breath. But it hurt to breathe. This impossible situation had escalated into a nightmare of epic proportions and she was drowning, being pulled down into the center of a black hole from which she might never emerge. Alec was free to return to his own world. Old house condemned. Mission accomplished.

Early the next morning Alec left as he'd said he would, taking Scotty with him. Hearing the child's cries of "but why, Daddy?" and his tearful pleading to please let him stay had almost been Shea's undoing. She'd finally run out to the barn, unable to bear hearing his cries, unwilling to watch them walk out the door forever.

When she eventually returned, the house was silent, as though it knew its time had come, awaiting annihilation like a condemned man awaiting his execution.

The merriment and laughter of Scotty's voice no longer echoed through the halls. But Alec's absence was the hardest to bear. She didn't cry because she couldn't. The numbness wouldn't let her.

Finally, on the third day, she saddled one of the horses. All her life, she'd found solace in the land. It had been a refuge where she could work through problems that seemed far greater than she could possibly contend with alone. Other than her dad dying, losing her home was the greatest hardship she'd ever faced. And the loss of the man she loved, however convoluted that might have been, was earth shattering.

She swung her leg over the saddle, gathered the reins and urged the mare toward the piney woods and the old homestead beyond. She knew going there would renew the memories of the last time she'd been there—with Alec.

The gentle, even stride of the mare was soothing as she carried Shea through the trees and over the meadows. The call of a red-tailed hawk as it circled overhead seemed to mock the fact she was alone. After dismounting, Shea walked to the sacred ground where five generations of her ancestors lay in eternal sleep. Stopping in front of the grave of William Morreston, she wished she could ask him so many questions.

Eventually, she made her way to the old homestead. As she looked at the burned-out hull, she could visualize Alec's face, hear his laugh and feel his arms around her. As the sun set on the horizon, Shea curled up on the edge of the old floorboards a mere foot from the spot where they had made love, and succumbed to the pain shredding her heart into tiny pieces. Unable to hold back her misery any longer, the heartache broke through any lingering restraints and sobs of loss ran rampant through her body.

Twelve

It had been almost a week since Alec had left the Bar H to take Scotty back to New York. Now, en route back to Dallas, he still didn't know what he could say to make Shea understand her safety was his primary concern.

He'd known he needed to get Scotty to a neutral setting. The child didn't need to witness the argument that was sure to take place when Alec went back to the ranch and her hardheaded resistance collided with his single-minded determination that she leave there before she was injured. Or worse.

The onboard office was furnished with the latest computers and advanced communication technology, enabling him to conduct business from anywhere in the world. Anything and everything needed to handle virtually any crisis was at his fingertips.

Except the one named Shea Hardin-Morreston.

His fingers drummed impatiently on the desktop as he gazed out the small window at the darkening sky. He was used to long flights, usually working his way from destination to destination, continent to continent. It helped to pass the time. But on this flight, he was incapable of concentrating on anything except Shea and that damned old house.

Shea's refusal to accept the reality of the situation and see the futility of what she wanted made no sense. It was not just the issue of the house. This was about the safety of a woman he'd come to care about very much. She'd opened a door to a place he'd long forgotten, reminding him of the things he'd loved as a boy. A feeling of peace had surrounded him at the ranch, encouraging him to set aside the abstract world to which he'd become accustomed. It had been a free fall out of the rat race into a new reality of home and heart; he had taken a step back to the things and the people that mattered. And he wanted Shea to be part of his new reality. He'd not imagined it without her. But if she didn't care enough to trust him...if she wasn't willing to let go of the past and take a chance on a future with him, then both of them would lose.

Suddenly, visions of his first wife clouded Alec's mind. Sondra had also wanted it all. The big house, the expensive cars had never been enough. She'd continued the affairs, the parties, the drugs, even after she'd learned she was pregnant, because that had been what had suited her. She'd pushed aside her own safety and the safety of their innocent child for her own selfish wants. And Shea was doing the same thing.

Shea's drug was the ranch. It was as addictive to her as drugs had been to Sondra. Shea was attempting to make him conform, get him to spend millions to put the house back in working order, and then... He didn't want to speculate on what she would do then.

God, he wanted to be wrong about Shea. His feelings for her ran deep. He'd actually let himself envision a future together and he'd never thought he would feel that way about any woman again.

Surely, by now Shea must have accepted the truth that the house wasn't safe. But still, he had to acknowledge it was her home. It was the only one she'd ever known. As she'd said when he issued the ultimatum to get out of that building, the ranch was her life. It defined who she was. At least in her mind. To Alec, she was so much more.

Hopefully the time he'd been away had given Shea a chance to calm down, to realize that things had to change.

Even so, convincing her to leave her home would take every amount of skill he possessed. She had to understand he wasn't forcing her out because of that damned contract. It was for her safety. It was because he cared. He didn't have a clue how it had happened, but he could no longer deny that truth. He was in love with Shea Hardin.

The issue of the land remained a black cloud over both their heads. It continued to drive a wedge between them and that had to end. If he had to choose between giving up the entire project and losing Shea, the project was history. He'd never thought a woman like Shea existed, let alone that he would find her. She had taken away all the suspicions and internal rage that had burned a hole in his soul for five long years, and opened his heart to the possibility of a future of happiness. She'd made him whole again. He was not about to lose her. Not over this land. Not over anything.

He glanced again at his watch. Ten minutes later than the last time he'd looked. Still half an hour out from Dallas-Fort Worth. He wanted to pace, needed some way to let off the tension churning in his gut. He'd never felt this uneasy, never sensed the need to hurry as he did now.

I never should have left without her. That thought kept churning in his mind. *I never should have left her alone in that house.*

Once the jet landed at the airport, a helicopter was waiting, ready to take him back to Calico Springs. This time he would make her listen to him. At the meeting he'd scheduled to take place in four days, he was calling a halt to the project. It was worth any financial loss if it meant having Shea in his life. He needed her. Scotty needed her. And he believed Shea needed them.

The sound seemed to come from far away. Shea ignored it, not wanting to leave the dark recesses of sleep that had finally given her temporary peace.

Almost every day since Alec and Scotty had left, she'd saddled a horse and had come out to the ruins of the old homestead. She'd reflected on her limited options but unlike the previous times in her life, she'd found no solution. There was no peace. In the end, everything came back to Alec and what she would do without him in her life.

The sound grew louder, now joined by a voice calling her name. Blinking open her eyes, she sat up.

Thunder rolled across the sky as lightning flashed, challenging the darkness. The wind roared around the old structure, bringing the smell of the pending rain.

"Shea!"

It was Hank. As she stood up, she saw the truck about a hundred yards away heading toward her at a high rate of speed. He came to a screeching halt in front of the foundation.

"There's trouble," he told her without preamble. "Get in."

Recognizing the serious tone in his voice, she jumped into the vehicle without a word. He spun around on two wheels and they headed back over the rise.

"What?" She was almost afraid to ask.

"It's the house," Hank said. "It's on fire."

"What!" Shea couldn't immediately grasp the meaning of what he said. "The house…*my* house?"

She saw him nod, his mouth set in a grim line.

"How?" Her mind was reeling.

"Don't know," he yelled over the sound of the racing engine. "My guess is lightning. But as old as the place is, it won't take it long to burn down. That wood's like dry kindling."

Shea sat in stunned silence. Hank bypassed the trail and shot a straight line for the house, tearing through the wooded area a half mile away from it. They bounced over stumps and plunged through shallow ravines, sideswiping trees and boulders.

As soon as they topped the last rise, she could see the flames against the darkened sky. Fire equipment surrounded the house along with police and ambulance. Men were running in all directions, shouting to each other and scrambling to battle the flames shooting out the windows. A black wall of smoke engulfed the old composite roof; the large streams of water the firefighters were spraying onto its burning surface had little effect. Bright red, blue and white lights flashed and cast an eerie ambiance over the horrific scene unfolding around her.

She jumped from the truck before Hank came to a complete stop and ran toward the house. One of the firefighters caught her, bringing her to a stop.

"I'm sorry, ma'am, but you'll need to stay back."

"It's my house," she screamed over the commotion.

"Ma'am, you can't go inside." His tone had changed to one of understanding, but he remained adamant in his refusal to let her near the house.

"But—"

"Please, ma'am, you must stay back. The walls could collapse at any time. Please."

She turned away, unable to stop the flow of tears as they streamed down her face. She'd never felt so powerless in her life. The nightmare was coming true, playing out in full color right in front of her eyes. She stumbled to the far side of the three-story structure and watched helplessly as the flames continued to eat at the roof.

At least Alec and Scotty were gone and in no danger.

Then something caught her attention. It looked like a face in the upstairs window. Scotty's room. She brushed the tears from her eyes and looked again. Was Alec here? Had they come back? Was Scotty trapped inside? Between the darkness and the smoke billowing out of the window, she couldn't be sure. Sheer terror gripped her heart. She anxiously searched around her for any sign of Alec.

"Scotty!" Firefighters were pulling more hoses from the trucks, yelling instructions to each other while the anxious ranch hands and their families looked on. Then in the distance, on the very edge of the illumination from the flashing lights on the emergency vehicles, she spotted a white car. It looked like the sedan Alec had been driving while he was here. He'd come back! Frantically, she took one more look around her but couldn't spot Alec in all the chaos. Time was running out. She ran to the closest firefighter, tugged on his jacket to get his attention and pointed to the upstairs window. "There is a child up there."

She had to yell to be heard over the roar of the fire and the commotion on the ground. The man looked in the direction she indicated. A dark cloud of smoke still plumed out the open window.

"I don't see anyone, ma'am," he said, still looking. "We checked the house before the fire got to this stage. There was no one inside."

"But he's there!" She pointed to the window.

The man turned and hurried back to one of the fire trucks, yelling instructions to the others. She didn't have time to wait. Scotty didn't have time to wait. Without another thought Shea took off at a dead run toward the kitchen door. If she hurried, there was a chance she could reach Scotty in time.

Taking a deep breath, she bounded up the outside steps and pushed her way inside. The wall of heat was overwhelming. A thick blanket of smoke filled the room, whirling around her as the fresh air followed her into the kitchen. She quickly wet some towels, held them against her face, and ran for the stairs, taking them two at a time. The closer she got to the second floor, the more intense the heat became, surrounding her like a giant furnace.

As she reached the top of the stairwell, she heard a loud crackling sound and a cloud of dark gray smoke billowed

down from the roof. She coughed violently as she urged
herself forward. Just a few steps more.

"Scotty!" No reply. Crouching low to the floor, she
crawled down the hall. The towels seemed of little help as
the smoke burned her throat and lungs. The loud roaring
from the inferno brought renewed terror. *Am I already too
late?* The smoke burned her eyes, further restricting her
sight. Feeling her way along the wall, she finally reached
his room.

She hesitated in the doorway only a fraction of a second
before plunging into the smoke and ash, not stopping until
she reached the window where she'd seen the small face.
Suddenly, the smoke swirled away from the open window.
She gasped for a breath of air. It was then she saw it. *The
owl.* It hadn't been Scotty she'd seen in the window. It was
his stuffed owl. At that instant, a loud crash from another
part of the house rocked the floor under her feet.

Turning, she began the arduous journey back down the
hall. Approaching the doorway to her old room, she knew
a moment of anguish for all the cherished things that would
soon be lost forever. The linens, hand-embroidered by her
mother, the wedding gown, pictures of her father and the
family Bible. The only things left of the Hardin family
were in that cedar chest. It sat not more than four feet from
where she stood. She couldn't see it because of the smoke,
but she knew it was there.

Acting purely on impulse, she lunged for the big chest.
Grabbing the handle, she began pulling it from the room.

The smoke was thicker than it had been only a few moments ago and every breath was a horrific struggle. At the
top of the stairs, she gave a hard push and the chest began
to slide down, bumping over each step. It was almost to the
bottom landing when the corner caught in the stair railing,
halting its progress.

Climbing over the chest, she tried tugging from the

lower side. Suddenly, the railing gave way and the chest lurched forward. The motion threw her off balance and she fell, tumbling the rest of the way down the stairs, the heavy trunk crashing down on top of her.

As she teetered on the edge of consciousness, she pushed at the trunk, but it had become lodged between the newel post and the wall, effectively pinning her underneath.

Her ears were ringing. With each cough, her lungs filled with more minuscule particles of ash. She pushed frantically at the chest, trying to dislodge it enough so she could scoot out from underneath.

The roar of the fire, which now surrounded her, was almost deafening. It was so hot. For a moment, she gave up her attempts to push the chest away and covered her face with her one free arm, desperately trying to breathe. Unable to move, all she could do was look toward the ceiling as the nightmare continued to unfold.

She knew she was suffocating, dying a horrendously slow death. Her thoughts were of Alec, her mind encapsulating their time together. He was a good person. A good father. And she loved him with all her heart. Even if that love wasn't returned. The times he'd held her in his arms she'd been given a little taste of heaven on earth. She could see his handsome face in her mind's eye. His smile. The glitter of amusement in his golden eyes. She could hear his voice, so strong and deep. She was glad she'd had the opportunity to know him. To know what it was like to totally lose herself in his arms. What she wouldn't give for another chance to be with him without the issue of the land hanging over their heads.

There was so much more to life than history and tradition. Alec had shown her that. The really important things were the people you loved, not man-made structures. Even the land couldn't give you a glimpse of the stars and hold you close and protect when you floated slowly back down

to earth. Material things couldn't make you feel safe while
a storm of trouble threatened to tear your life apart. They
couldn't give you hope for the future. They couldn't love
you back. Why hadn't she realized it before it was too late?
The way she missed her dad should have told her it was the
people you love that mattered.

Tears slipped from the corners of her eyes. She could
barely feel the moisture running down her face. It was so
hot. If only she had a second chance she would make sure
Alec knew he was the only thing that really mattered. Oh,
how she wished she could somehow let him know.

"I love you Alec," she whispered as more tears joined
the first. "I love you." Another crash pulled her attention
to the area behind her. Craning her neck, she watched helplessly as pieces of flaming debris fell all around.

The thick cloud of smoke prevented her from seeing the
flames on the burning ceiling above her, but she heard the
loud cracking of the fire and the deafening shriek of the
timbers as they lost their centuries-old struggle to hold up
the roof. She heard her own scream, but it was lost in the
loud crashing of falling timber. Then blackness swirled
inside her head, dragging her down into the blissful realm
of oblivion.

Almost as soon as the helicopter cleared the city lights
of Dallas, Alec detected a yellowish glow on the darkening
north horizon. It was a fire of some kind. While he prayed
the cause was a farmer clearing out a brush pile, a churning in his gut told him it could be the house at the Bar H.

"Chuck, can this thing go any faster?" Alec asked the
pilot through the headset.

The pilot nodded as if he sensed the urgency, sending
them plunging ahead into the darkness. The closer they got
to the yellowish glow, the more the fear churned in Alec's
gut. Finally he knew. It was the old house.

I never should have left her in that house.

Before the chopper fully set down in an area near the barn, Alec jumped out. The sight of the old, three-story house ablaze against the blackened sky was surreal. His worst fears were confirmed. The firefighters swarmed around the structure, sending streams of water to the top and sides in a last-ditch effort to save even a portion of the building.

Alec looked everywhere for Shea but she was not to be found. As the sky opened and the rain began to fall in torrents, he spotted Hank. The ranch foreman was standing beside the Jeep, helplessly watching the firefighters' valiant efforts to contain the fire.

He raced to the older man. "Where's Shea?" Placing his hand on Hank's shoulder, he spun him around. "Hank! Where is Shea?"

Frowning, the old cowboy looked around. "She was just here. One of the firemen pushed her back from the house."

A quick glance told Alec she was nowhere in sight. An ungodly fear began to fester in his gut.

"I don't know where she went..."

The scream that pierced the night air was a sound that would haunt Alec for the rest of his life. Above the shouts of the men, the roar of the fire and the rumbling thunder overhead, one shrill scream from inside the burning inferno gave him his answer.

"My God, she's inside!" he whispered almost to himself. "Hank, Shea's inside. Get help!" He ran toward the house.

Before he could reach the porch, one of the firefighters grabbed his arm. "Sir, you can't go inside."

"She's in there. She's inside."

"Sir, no one is in the structure and we can't let you go—"

With one well-placed blow of his fist, Alec halted both the man's words and any further attempt to hold him back.

He sprang for the kitchen door, sensing others close behind who might try to stop him.

At first he didn't see her. The combination of searing heat, black swirling smoke and the demands from the firemen to get out almost made him turn away. Then Alec spied the chest at the bottom of the stairs and the still form lying underneath it. For an instant terror flooded his body and the vile churning of his stomach rendered him incapable of movement.

"There!" he shouted and lunged in that direction.

The men pulled the chest from over Shea's limp form. Alec scooped her body into his arms and ran for the door. A loud crash followed their retreat as the roof tumbled to the ground behind them.

Once he was clear of the building, Alec fell to his knees and laid her gently on the water-soaked earth.

Immediately, paramedics and firefighters surrounded her. One of them pushed him up against a fire truck and shoved an oxygen mask over his face, while the others focused their attention on Shea's still body.

The downpour continued as the lightning pierced the clouds overhead. For what seemed an eternity, Alec could only watch in stunned disbelief while the paramedics worked to bring life back to her fragile body. He ignored the rain, the fire, the shouts of the firefighters, every cell in his body attuned to the woman who was fighting for her life.

Finally, a small cough gave him some hope. She was alive. But she'd been in the smoke a long time. Maybe too long.

Within twenty minutes, EMTs had Shea strapped in and the Care Flight chopper lifted off, heading for the special burn unit at Regency Hospital in Dallas. Alec wasn't allowed to ride with her, but he followed in his own helicopter.

Shea was already being treated when he entered the ER. She was alive, but no one could tell him anything more than that. He called Leona. And he waited.

Two hours later, one of the doctors walked into the hallway.

"Mr. Morreston? I'm Dr. Clements. Your wife is stable, but we're going to keep her a few days just as a precautionary measure. She may have a few bruises, but considering the circumstances that brought her here, I'd have to say she was very lucky. The concern is her lungs. She has some indication of thermal injury to her upper airway and depending on the toxicity of the wood, it may take another forty-eight hours for any chemical injuries to become evident. We want to be sure she's okay before she's released."

With a comforting tap on his arm, the doctor left and Alec was once again alone with nothing but a handful of hope and a gut full of regrets to keep him company. He didn't want to think about what might have happened had he not returned when he had. He revisited that narrow escape in his mind a thousand times before the sun peeked over the far horizon.

Three days later, Shea and Alec made the ride in the limo from the hospital to the large hotel on the Dallas outskirts in silence. He sat beside her as he had in the hospital room. Not pushing her to talk, just silently offering his strength.

Shea was grateful to be alive. The fact that Alec was here with her tugged at her heart. They would have to talk eventually. She had to make sure he knew she would not make any further attempt to keep the land. It was his land, after all, and had been from the beginning. After everything she'd put him through, eating crow seemed the least she could do.

She'd been given the second chance she'd prayed for.

She had to use it carefully. She would not screw up again. Every cell in her body wanted nothing more than to fall into his arms and confess how very much she loved him. But while in the hospital, she hadn't been able to stop thinking about their situation, and it had occurred to her that a full confession of her feelings might not be the best way to go.

Apparently Alec had returned to the Bar H, no doubt intending to make sure she'd packed her bags. He hadn't counted on the house burning down. Rather than simply escorting her to the door, he'd been forced to save her from her own foolishness. It was bad enough that he'd risked his life for her; now her immediate homeless status effectively made her a liability. Again.

She wasn't sure how to approach him. Declaring her love could be awkward for him and cause him to feel responsible for her welfare. This was her last chance, her *only* chance, to get it right. She had to be strong, this time for Alec.

When the bellhop opened the door to the luxury suite, Shea glanced around at the opulent surroundings. Never could she have imagined such luxury. It suddenly washed over her: this was Alec's world. After his time at the ranch, she'd come to think of him not as a billionaire but just a nice, if somewhat stubborn, guy. Being here, seeing a sample of how he must usually live was…surreal.

She walked across the wide living area to the wall of glass that overlooked the vast expanse of Dallas.

"Are you hungry?" Alec inquired from behind her.

She shook her head. "No. But I would dearly love a bath."

"To your left through that door, Mrs. Morreston." A man in a hotel uniform stood just inside the doorway to the suite. "Please, allow me to draw it for you. How do you like the water?"

While Shea groped for an answer, Alec interjected, "Very warm. Thanks." When the man disappeared into the next room, Alec looked at her, his eyes glittering with amusement. "Hopefully you'll have plenty of hot water."

She couldn't help but return his smile. He was referring to the night Scotty had used all the hot water and she'd had to finish her shower in the icy tap from the well. In frustration she'd then gone after a sleeping Alec with a pillow.

"You'll find some clothes in the closet and bureau. I left it up to the salesclerk to send over what you'd need until you can replenish your wardrobe. If she missed something, let me know."

"Thanks."

The master bedroom was as spacious as the vast living area. It had the same wall of glass offering the million-dollar view, only it was dominated by a huge bed draped with silken linens so thick and luxurious it looked as if a person could completely disappear into the softness when she lay down.

The dressing room and bath were just beyond it. Shea was quite certain the oval tub could hold ten people. At least.

She emerged an hour later feeling clean and pampered and smelling of lilacs. Dressed in one of the comfortable new white T-shirts from the bureau, she walked directly to the bed and climbed in.

Exhaustion pulled her into sleep. She had a vague awareness that Alec joined her sometime in the night. His strong arms pulled her close, offering his warmth and security.

The rays of the morning sun filtered softly through the sheer draperies. Shea opened her eyes, remembering immediately where she was and all that had happened. On the far corner of the bed she spotted a deep red rose with a note underneath it. After picking up the beautiful flower, she inhaled the rich perfumed aroma, then grabbed the small piece of paper.

*Knew you needed to rest so I didn't wake you. I'm in
a meeting downstairs.*

   *Coffee and juice on the side table. Back as soon
as I can.*
-Alec

He had no need to hurry. As far as his plans for the
ranch, he would have to wait while she cleared the land of
several employees—some of whom lived on the ranch—
the horses and roughly three thousand head of cattle. It
wouldn't happen overnight. In fact, she didn't quite know
where to begin. But now that this stumbling block over
ownership had been resolved, Alec could get back to his
life and somehow she would have to find a way to get on
with hers. Wherever that would be. Whatever it entailed.

Fanning through the new clothes that hung in the huge
closet, she selected a simple yet elegant dress in robin's
egg blue. There were some pumps with the name Trump
in gold lettering on the insole.

As she sipped a cup of delicious coffee delivered by a
hotel employee, she sat back and looked out over the city
of Dallas, her mind on Alec and what to say to him before
she left. It would be painful to say goodbye. She loved him
so much. But she would not be one of those women who
clung to men who didn't want them. Leaving was the right
thing to do. The only thing to do. Maybe he'd stop by and
say hello if his business ever brought him back to the area.
The tears welled in her eyes but she forced them back. This
time, for Alec, she had to be strong.

By late afternoon she needed a new space. She was not
used to sitting idle. Around two, Alec called to explain he
would be tied up for a while longer. She assured him there
was no hurry and went out to explore the hotel on her own.

With a soft ding, the elevator door opened to the mar-
bled lobby. Stepping out, she immediately noticed a large

flat-screen television mounted on the wall behind the concierge's stand. It listed the various shops and meeting rooms and the locations of each. Beneath the Presidential Suite, one name stood out: Morreston.

A chill ran down her spine. Could this be the meeting Alec had mentioned about the development of the ranch? Without any conscious thought, she began making her way in that direction. After rounding the far corner, she took a small escalator up to the next level.

The royal-blue carpeted reception area was deserted. Her hands clenched into fists as she walked silently to the meeting room entrance and pulled open one of the mahogany doors. Immediately she was assailed with the buzz of conversation. About forty men and women filled the room. Some held flutes of champagne while others sipped coffee. Most stood in smaller groups, nodding or arguing some point they were trying to make. But the mood throughout the entire room was excitement.

Stepping inside, she searched for Alec, finally spotting him in the far corner. Like the other men in the room, he wore a dark suit and tie. From the way it fit, no doubt it was custom tailored and probably cost more than the ranch. Surrounded by eight or nine people, his hands moved as he emphasized the point he was making.

The churning in her stomach made her feel queasy. This was it. The meeting. And these were the people, the investors, who'd put up millions to develop the Bar H, putting their faith in Alec to give them America's grandest entertainment complex for their vested interest.

He was at home in this setting. So confident. So self-assured. These people were accomplished in their own right, yet they held Alec and his capabilities high on a pedestal, clinging to his every word. The more that realization sank in, the smaller she felt.

A white-jacketed waiter appeared next to her, offering

glasses of champagne on a silver tray. She shook her head in polite refusal. What was she doing here? Had she honestly thought something good would come of the affair with Alec? And clearly, that's all it had been. At least to him.

Her eyes fell on a large display table in the center of the room. She knew it was a scale model rendering of the future of the ranch. Strangely, she didn't care to look any closer. It no longer mattered. Alec would probably direct the project from his office in New York. When this meeting ended, Alec would be gone.

Tears stung her eyes as her entire body began to tremble. Her heart pounded in her chest as she tried to swallow back the nausea churning in her stomach. She thought she'd been prepared to accept the eventuality of his leaving and say goodbye with an understanding smile, keeping the agony of regret hidden deep inside. She hadn't foreseen that the pain of losing him would be so horrific. Now she had to wonder how she would ever get through this.

Feeling lost in the din of voices, she took one last glance toward Alec. A man separated himself from the others, placed his hand on Alec's arm and nodded in her direction. For an instant, their eyes met before the world tilted and the room began to spin.

Shea turned, making her way back to the lobby, away from the meeting room before her tears fell and she embarrassed Alec in front of his colleagues.

The elevator doors immediately opened when she pressed the button. As she stumbled inside, she heard Alec's voice calling her name.

"Shea!"

His deep voice exploded into the hotel suite. Despite the emotions running rampant, her heart still responded to the sound of his voice. Hastily she swiped the tears from her face.

"They have it wrong." He spoke to her from the bedroom doorway. "That scale model is not even close to what I intended. A few of the investors have a tendency to push things to the limit. What you saw is not going to happen."

"It's okay." Shea nodded and began folding the few items of clothing Alec had bought for her. There had been too many harsh words between them, too much pain, too many regrets in the few months they'd been together. She hadn't even seen the model. She hadn't wanted to look. Alec had already told her the way of life as she'd known it was over. The old house burning down had underscored his point. Changing the scale model wouldn't change anything. It wouldn't change how she felt about him. It wouldn't make him stay. She just needed it all to stop, needed this insane emotional roller coaster to come to a permanent end.

"It doesn't matter," she replied quietly, calmly. "It's your land. You can do with it whatever you want."

"Shea—"

She shook her head and forced a smile as she placed the remaining personal items in the small designer sack that would serve as a suitcase, holding all she had left in the world. Lifting it from the bed and pasting on a brave smile, she turned to face Alec. "Congratulations on your project. I mean that. I'm sure your venture will be a huge success. Your investors have confidence in you. They know you're the best."

She had to accept Alec would be leaving and never coming back. She knew once this was a done deal, the restraints of the old lease over and forgotten, she would never see him again. Fresh tears threatened to fall but she determinedly held them in check.

"Someday, if you're back in this area for any reason, be sure and stop—" She couldn't finish. She couldn't tell him to stop by and say hello. She had no idea where she would be. "Stop by Leona's. She'll know where to find me."

For a long moment, Alec watched her. He opened his mouth as though he wanted to say something, then apparently thought better of it. For that she was grateful. The only thing left was admitting her love for the man who stood so tall, so handsome in front of her. But she wouldn't do that. She would not push him from one awkward situation into another. She respected him too much to do that.

Then suddenly Alec moved, grabbing her arms and spinning her around so her back was against the wall. His lips were hard, almost cruel when they came down on hers. Hungrily, he took her mouth, consuming hers with a passion that threatened to devour her very soul. There was no gentleness this time, just raw need. And she gloried in the strength of him, the taste of him. She kissed him back with all the pent-up longing that had been tearing her apart for days, silently conveying her need for him. *One last time. One final glimpse of heaven in his arms.*

The thin straps of the dress prevented him from touching her. With little effort he dispensed with them and roughly pushed the dress to the floor. His hands cupped her bare breasts, molding them, kneading them, feeling them expand under his touch while his mouth continued to ravish hers. His mouth left her lips, kissing and nipping a path to her neck, then lower to suck the swollen buds of her breasts. She trembled, her hand fisted in his hair, holding him to her.

His hand slid down across her stomach, then lower, to the sensitive area between her legs. The surge of passion at his touch pushed her hips against his hand, confirming her need. Alec quickly removed the thin scrap of lace and stroked her. She moaned at his touch.

She heard Alec let out a low growl.

"I can't go slow," he rasped against her ear, his voice rough.

"I don't…want you…to."

He unfastened his pants just enough, then lifted her, positioning her to receive him. Without a second's pause, he pushed deep inside.

His hungry mouth swallowed her soft moans as her body strove to accommodate him, to accept and embrace him and the heated force that drove him. It was as though he needed to brand her as his. If only that were true. She wrapped her legs around his hips, holding him to her as he began to move, driving any coherent thought from her mind. His muscles hardened as he pounded into her, taking her hard, filling her.

"Oh, Alec. I'm…" She didn't finish the sentence, but he knew.

Grasping her hips, he pushed even deeper, again and again, until she cried out as her passion exploded. The final waves of her climax caught Alec in the storm of emotion and he followed her, pulsating deep inside her as he growled her name.

As the waves of passion subsided, she cupped the back of his head, smoothed the damp tendrils of his hair, kissed his neck and under his chin while he fought for breath.

"I love you, Alec," she said softly. "Forgive me, but I love you."

He raised his head and his eyes found hers. "Shea," he murmured her name, then kissed her again, passionately, silently sealing the bond between them.

He swung her into his arms. Without a word, he carried her into the bedroom, placing her on the soft mattress. Quickly shedding his clothes, he lay down next to her, pulling her close.

Her head resting on his broad chest, she listened to the strong beat of his heart. She was still reeling from his lovemaking and the fact he was here with her instead of at his meeting.

"What do you remember?"

She closed her eyes. She didn't want to do this. Not now.

She hadn't figured out exactly what to say to him. But she answered truthfully. "Everything."

"Why did you go into the house?" His hand played in the fine strands of her hair.

"I…thought I saw Scotty. Upstairs. In his bedroom window. I thought you'd brought him back." She pulled away and looked at him through the pale city light filtering into the room. "I couldn't find you in all the chaos, but maybe if I hurried, I could save him. When I got to his room, I realized it was his stuffed owl that I'd seen from outside. As I was running back to the stairs, I remembered the chest. I thought I could save it."

She lay back on her pillow, covering her face as the somber weight of total loss returned. "It was all I had…from my mother, the only pictures of my dad. After our wedding, when I folded Mom's gown and put it back in the chest, I thought it would be a safe place." Swallowing hard, she turned her gaze to Alec. "Why did you come back? How did you…? I don't understand."

"I intended to make sure you got out of the house before something happened. My timing could have been better. I was on my way back and saw the flames." A rueful smile touched his lips. "I'd anticipated evicting you would be a major hurdle, but I never anticipated having to carry you out unconscious."

She drew in a sharp but shaky breath. There was her answer. He had just eliminated any lingering hope. When Alec had asked her how much she remembered, it included his demand that she leave. And he'd just confirmed he'd meant it.

It had all, finally, come to an end.

In the slender moments before the light of a new day began to appear in the eastern sky, Shea made her way quietly through the suite and toward the door, glancing one last time at the sleeping man on the bed. He had come into her life so unexpectedly. But in the end, he'd given her so much more than he would take away. Now it was her turn to give him the freedom he needed to go forward with his life. And somehow, maybe, someday she could get on with hers.

Thirteen

The week she spent with Leona provided some time and space for Shea to try to work through all the emotions and grief eating away at her soul. Leona gave her plenty of room and didn't try to encourage her to talk but made sure Shea knew she was there for her if or when she needed her.

Alec had called every day, checking to be sure she was all right. She'd heard Leona assuring him that Shea would be fine. It was good to know somebody thought so.

This morning, Shea felt the time had come. The day dawned bright and beautiful, and she knew she'd avoided returning to the ranch long enough. She had to take the next step in saying goodbye. Had to deal with the memories of when she'd been happy, her heart full of hope.

She thanked Leona for her offer to accompany her, but this was something Shea had to do on her own. With quiet understanding, Leona held out the keys to her truck.

The site where the house had stood for so many years had been cleared, all remains of the old structure removed and the ground leveled. Parts of the small path that at one time had led from the kitchen door through the small back yard and out to the main barn were still visible. All of the various ranch buildings were intact. Only the house was missing.

She slowly followed the path across the yard and into the hallway of the main barn. The familiar scents of freshly cut alfalfa, leather and pine shavings filled the air. She stopped to stroke the silky necks of the horses housed inside. When she got to Ransom's stall, memories flooded her mind and pain gripped her heart anew. The day Alec had ridden the spirited animal to the old homestead. The small campfire where they'd talked and laughed and shared the meal Hank had prepared for them.

The rain.

The night that had followed.

Forcing herself away from the stall, she ambled on toward the tack room. Before she reached it, her eyes fell on an object that looked incredibly familiar. Sitting against the wall on the floor was what appeared to be the old trunk. But that was impossible. It had been destroyed in the fire. Frowning, she reached down and touched the top, almost afraid it would disappear. But it was real. The marks of fire damage were apparent on the top and sides, but overall, it was in remarkably good condition.

Immediately falling to her knees, she pushed open the lid. A faint pine scent touched her senses. Removing the layer of tissue paper she saw the family pictures. *How did they get here?*

Beneath the photographs were her mother's hand-embroidered linens followed by the two quilts bearing the initials A.H., and, finally, the wedding gown. She swallowed hard as she gently reached in, picked up the dress and held it to her heart. Alec was behind this. Somehow, he'd managed to save it all.

Memories of her holding the dress in front of her, trying to decide if she should wear it to their wedding, flashed through her mind. Tears burned the backs of her eyes. She was glad she'd worn it. With a sad smile, she gently folded the dress, intending to return it to the trunk. Then she noticed a loose board on the bottom. Frowning, she set the gown on the quilts and removed the thin piece of wood.

Beneath it…letters. Dozens of letters. Really old, yellowed with age. *What are these?* Picking up the one on top, she began to read.

> *April 12, 1814*
> *My Dearest Alyssa, My Beloved...*

They all were signed William Morreston. Alec's great-great-grandfather.

Glancing over the words, she quickly saw they were love letters. Another look inside the trunk and Shea saw an old photo among the letters. The tin-plated picture had two images: a young woman standing beside a tall, handsome man.

Suddenly, she knew what these were, the pieces falling together like parts of a puzzle. William Morreston had courted Alyssa Hardin, daughter of the widow, Mary Hardin. He'd courted her, fallen in love with her and they had planned to marry. Photographs were rare and costly back in those days. It had to have been taken for a very special occasion. Such as a wedding. The quilts, the linens...this trunk had been Alyssa's hope chest. And it was Alyssa who had perished in the fire at the old homestead. Before she could become William's wife.

One thought exploded inside her head: it had never been about the land. The contract written two hundred years ago, the clause that forced her and Alec to marry, all of it had been intended to bring two ancestors of William and Alyssa together.

It had been about Alec. All along, it had been about him.

An invisible hand gripped her heart. She couldn't breathe. Her body began to tremble as she tried to blink back the tears. But they fell down her face, dropping onto the letters clutched in her hand. Even though she'd left Alec with the best intentions, she'd walked out nonetheless. And even though he'd called to check on her, he wouldn't be back. That truth slammed into her like an airbag deploying in an unforeseen crash. He was gone. Forever. The pain in her heart was unbearable, the sadness so deep, so piercing she knew she would never recover.

Through eyes blurred with tears, she looked at the sparkling wedding ring on her left hand. It seemed like a lifetime ago, the night Alec had slipped it back on her finger and told her to never take it off. At the time, she'd counted the days until her twelve-month sentence would be over, when she would be free of him and could happily throw the ring in his face. But it had become a part of her, as had the man who'd given it to her. Subconsciously she'd never let go of the hope she and Alec could work things out. Now, she faced the grim truth.

She'd failed to keep the greatest gift that fate could bestow from slipping through her fingers. She'd lost the greatest man—the *only* man she had ever loved and would ever love as long as she lived. A man who but for a ridiculous clause in a two-hundred-year-old contract, never would have entered her life.

The tears streamed unchecked down her face and she had no will to hold them back as another wave of misery overwhelmed her. The tears blurred the image of the beautiful ring as she began to slide it from her hand. If only…

"I told you to leave that ring where it is," said a deep familiar voice from behind her.

With a gasp, Shea whirled around. Alec stood just inside the barn, looking big and rugged and entirely too handsome. Dressed in jeans and a white cotton T-shirt, he stood with one hand resting on a stall door, the other on his hip.

It took her a few seconds to find her voice. "Alec? What… what are you doing here? What do you…?"

"What do I want?" he asked, stepping away from the stall, his arms falling to his side. "I want to go back in time where the past few weeks never happened. I want to hold my wife in my arms every night and see her face when I wake up the next morning. Emphasis on seeing her the next morning."

She knew he was referring to the hotel in Dallas when she'd snuck out to come home.

"And I want to see her belly grow with my son or daughter." She noted a flare in his golden eyes at those words. His mouth then pulled into a serious line. "I've shelved the entire project, Shea. My stipulation to continue is it will be built completely across the river in Oklahoma. I don't intend for one rock, one blade of grass, one single drop of water to be disturbed on this ranch. I've spent the last week making damn sure that doesn't happen. If the investors go for it, good enough. If not—" he shrugged his broad shoulders "—I really don't give a damn. Nothing is worth losing you."

A frown crossed his face, his eyes conveying the seriousness of his words, and for countless moments, neither moved. "Why did you leave the hotel? Have I lost you, Shea?"

Shaking her head, she rose to her feet. "You could never lose me, Alec. I love you too much."

Then she was in his arms—strong, powerful arms that were gentle as he held her tightly against him. She gazed into eyes the color of topaz as he cupped her face and wiped away the tears with his thumbs. His lips, hot and oh so incredible, covered hers and she surrendered to the overwhelming love that had grown for this man in spite of all the reasons it shouldn't. The warmth and the feel and the taste of him filled her. The wonderful musky male scent of his skin surrounded her as his hard body pressed against hers. She kissed him back with all the love she had, the tears of misery changing to those of pure joy.

Finally, Alec raised his head, but stayed a mere breath away. She touched his face, amazed that she had a chance to love and be loved by such a man.

"Just so we're clear this time, I've been in love with you since the day you walked into Ben's office," Alec admitted as she looked into his eyes. "I admit I fought it, even after we were married. I told myself I was slitting my own throat, setting myself up for a hell of a fall because someone like you just didn't happen to someone like me. I can handle cutthroat tactics, lying, backstabbing from my adversaries, sometimes even my supporters. My world hasn't left much room for honesty and innocence. Trust is something new to me." His gaze traveled over her face. "But you've shown me I can trust again. I can love. And I love you, *Mrs. Morreston*, with everything I have inside me."

A glint of amusement flickered in his eyes, making Shea smile.

"You know, I think I might get used to that name."

"You'd better," Alec said, in a teasingly threatening tone. "Because you're stuck with it for the rest of your life."

She knew he was telling the truth. This man, this incredible man, truly loved her. He was her husband. Scotty was her son. And it didn't matter whether they lived in New York or Texas or someplace in between as long as they were together. That realization was sealed when Alec's lips again came down over hers in a deep, passionate embrace that left no doubts whatsoever.

His lips left hers, kissing his way to her ear. "Mmm." He growled and nuzzled her neck. "We need to be on our way back to Dallas."

"Back to Dallas?"

"Mmm. To the hotel. To the bedroom…"

Shea grinned, caught her bottom lip, and shook her head as she backed him through the open door of the tack room and toward the stack of blankets in the corner.

"That hotel is much too far away."

Alec's eyebrows rose, then a smile turned up the corners of his lips as he realized her intent and kicked the door closed behind them.

And there was no further talking for a very long time.

* * * * *

COMING NEXT MONTH FROM

HARLEQUIN

Desire

Available March 3, 2015

#2359 ROYAL HEIRS REQUIRED
Billionaires and Babies • by Cat Schield
Love and duty collide as Prince Gabriel Alessandro weds Lady Olivia Darcy to assume his nation's throne. But when he discovers he's the secret father of twin girls, will all bets be off?

#2360 MORE THAN A CONVENIENT BRIDE
Texas Cattleman's Club: After the Storm
by Michelle Celmer
What could be simpler than a marriage of convenience between friends? That's what star Texas surgeon Lucas Wakefield and researcher Julie Kingston think, until a jealous ex shows up and throws a wrench in their plans.

#2361 AT THE RANCHER'S REQUEST
Lone Star Legends • by Sara Orwig
It was a dark and stormy night when billionaire rancher Mike Calhoun rescued the stranded motorist. Now the widower has a storm in his own life as he's torn by unwanted attraction to this pregnant, vulnerable beauty...

#2362 AFTER HOURS WITH HER EX
by Maureen Child
When prodigal son Sam Wyatt comes home to his family's ski resort, he must work with his estranged wife to keep the business alive. But does this mean new life for the relationship he left behind?

#2363 PREGNANT BY THE SHEIKH
The Billionaires of Black Castle • by Olivia Gates
Numair can reclaim his birthright and gain the power of two thrones by marrying Jenan. And Jenan is more than willing to provide an heir for this delicious man—until she discovers his true agenda.

#2364 THE WEDDING BARGAIN
The Master Vintners • by Yvonne Lindsay
Shanal will sacrifice everything, even wed her unlovable boss, for her destitute parents' sakes. But when she gets cold feet at the altar, it's white knight Raif to the rescue. Will their desire be her redemption?

YOU CAN FIND MORE INFORMATION ON UPCOMING HARLEQUIN® TITLES, FREE EXCERPTS AND MORE AT WWW.HARLEQUIN.COM.

HDCNM0215

REQUEST YOUR FREE BOOKS!
2 FREE NOVELS PLUS 2 FREE GIFTS!

HARLEQUIN® *Desire*

ALWAYS POWERFUL, PASSIONATE AND PROVOCATIVE

YES! Please send me 2 FREE Harlequin Desire® novels and my 2 FREE gifts (gifts are worth about $10). After receiving them, if I don't wish to receive any more books, I can return the shipping statement marked "cancel." If I don't cancel, I will receive 6 brand-new novels every month and be billed just $4.55 per book in the U.S. or $4.99 per book in Canada. That's a savings of at least 13% off the cover price! It's quite a bargain! Shipping and handling is just 50¢ per book in the U.S. and 75¢ per book in Canada.* I understand that accepting the 2 free books and gifts places me under no obligation to buy anything. I can always return a shipment and cancel at any time. Even if I never buy another book, the two free books and gifts are mine to keep forever.

225/326 HDN F4ZC

Name	(PLEASE PRINT)
Address	Apt. #
City	State/Prov.	Zip/Postal Code

Signature (if under 18, a parent or guardian must sign)

Mail to the **Harlequin® Reader Service:**
IN U.S.A.: P.O. Box 1867, Buffalo, NY 14240-1867
IN CANADA: P.O. Box 609, Fort Erie, Ontario L2A 5X3

Want to try two free books from another line?
Call 1-800-873-8635 or visit www.ReaderService.com.

* Terms and prices subject to change without notice. Prices do not include applicable taxes. Sales tax applicable in N.Y. Canadian residents will be charged applicable taxes. Offer not valid in Quebec. This offer is limited to one order per household. Not valid for current subscribers to Harlequin Desire books. All orders subject to credit approval. Credit or debit balances in a customer's account(s) may be offset by any other outstanding balance owed by or to the customer. Please allow 4 to 6 weeks for delivery. Offer available while quantities last.

Your Privacy—The Harlequin® Reader Service is committed to protecting your privacy. Our Privacy Policy is available online at www.ReaderService.com or upon request from the Harlequin Reader Service.

We make a portion of our mailing list available to reputable third parties that offer products we believe may interest you. If you prefer that we not exchange your name with third parties, or if you wish to clarify or modify your communication preferences, please visit us at www.ReaderService.com/consumerschoice or write to us at Harlequin Reader Service Preference Service, P.O. Box 9062, Buffalo, NY 14269. Include your complete name and address.

"We'll have to kiss," she heard Luc say, and it took her
brain a second to catch up with her ears.

"Kiss?"

"During the wedding ceremony," he said.

"Oh, right." Julie hadn't considered that. She thought
about kissing Luc, and a peculiar little shiver cascaded
down the length of her spine. Back when she'd first met
him, she used to think about the two of them doing a lot
more than just kissing, but he had been too hung up on
Amelia and their recently broken engagement to even
think about another woman. So hung up that he'd left
his life in Royal behind and traveled halfway around the
world with Doctors Without Borders.

A recent dumpee herself, Julie had been just as con-
fused and vulnerable at the time, and she'd known there
would be nothing worse for her ego than a rebound

relationship. She and Luc were, and always would be, better off as friends.

"Is that a problem?" Luc asked.

She blinked. "Problem?"

"Us kissing. You got an odd look on your face."

Had she? "It's no problem at all," she assured him.

"We'll have to start acting like a married couple," he said. "You'll have to move in with me. But nothing in our relationship will change. We only have to make it look as if it has."

But by pretending, by making it look real to everyone else, wasn't that in itself a change to their relationship?

Ugh. She'd never realized how complicated this would be.

"Look," he said, frowning. "I want you to stay in the US, but if it's going to cause a rift in our friendship... Do you think it's worth it?"

"It is worth it. And I don't want you to think that I'm not grateful. I am."

"I know you are." He smiled and laid a hand on her forearm, and the feel of his skin against hers gave her that little shiver again.

What the heck was going on between them?

Don't miss
MORE THAN A CONVENIENT BRIDE
by Michelle Celmer, available March 2015 wherever
Harlequin® Desire books and ebooks are sold.

www.Harlequin.com